## The Teen Model Mystery

In the film studio, Nancy and Bess were talking to the director, when the telephone rang. Charmaine, the director's assistant, picked it up and said, "Festa Films, can I help you?"

Nancy noticed her hand suddenly clench the receiver. A moment later Charmaine hung up and turned to Nancy, her face set in an expression of shock.

"Who was it?" Nancy asked.

"I don't know," Charmaine said slowly. "But whoever it was, he told me to give you a message. He said that if you and Bess don't go home and mind your own business, you're going to get hurt . . . badly hurt!"

# Nancy Drew
# Mystery Stories

#58 The Flying Saucer Mystery
#62 The Kachina Doll Mystery
#72 The Haunted Carousel
#77 The Bluebeard Room
#79 The Double Horror of Fenley Place
#81 The Mardi Gras Mystery
#87 The Case of the Rising Stars
#89 The Case of the Disappearing Deejay
#91 The Girl Who Couldn't Remember
#92 The Ghost of Craven Cove
#93 The Case of the Safecracker's Secret
#94 The Picture-Perfect Mystery
#97 The Mystery at Magnolia Mansion
#98 The Haunting of Horse Island
#99 The Secret of Seven Rocks
#101 The Mystery of the Missing
   Millionairess
#103 The Stranger in the Shadows
#104 The Mystery of the Jade Tiger
#105 The Clue in the Antique Trunk
#106 The Case of the Artful Crime
#108 The Secret of the Tibetan Treasure
#109 The Mystery of the Masked Rider
#110 The Nutcracker Ballet Mystery
#111 The Secret at Solaire
#112 Crime at the Queen's Court
#113 The Secret Lost at Sea

#114 The Search for the Silver Persian
#115 The Suspect in the Smoke
#116 The Case of the Twin Teddy Bears
#117 Mystery on the Menu
#118 Trouble at Lake Tahoe
#119 The Mystery of the Missing Mascot
#120 The Case of the Floating Crime
#121 The Fortune-Teller's Secret
#122 The Message in the Haunted Mansion
#123 The Clue on the Silver Screen
#124 The Secret of the Scarlet Hand
#125 The Teen Model Mystery
#126 The Riddle in the Rare Book
#127 The Case of the Dangerous Solution
#128 The Treasure in the Royal Tower
#129 The Baby-sitter Burglaries
#130 The Sign of the Falcon
#131 The Hidden Inheritance
#132 The Fox Hunt Mystery
#133 The Mystery at the Crystal Palace
#134 The Secret of the Forgotten Cave
#135 The Riddle of the Ruby Gazelle
#136 The Wedding Day Mystery
#137 In Search of the Black Rose
#138 The Legend of the Lost Gold
#139 The Secret of Candlelight Inn
#140 The Door-to-Door Deception

## Available from MINSTREL Books

NANCY DREW MYSTERY STORIES®

## 125

# NANCY DREW®

## THE TEEN MODEL MYSTERY

### CAROLYN KEENE

A MINSTREL® BOOK

PUBLISHED BY POCKET BOOKS

New York  London  Toronto  Sydney  Tokyo  Singapore

A MINSTREL PAPERBACK *Original*

 A Minstrel Book published by
POCKET BOOKS, a division of Simon & Schuster Inc.
1230 Avenue of the Americas, New York, NY 10020

Copyright © 1995 by Simon & Schuster Inc.
Produced by Mega-Books, Inc.

ISBN: 0-671-87208-7

First Minstrel Books printing June 1995

10  9  8  7  6  5

Cover art by Aleta Jenks

Printed in the U.S.A.

# Contents

1   Set for Suspense                 1
2   Missing!                        10
3   Sabotage?                       19
4   Runaway Model                   30
5   Friends and Enemies             40
6   A Chase into Darkness           50
7   A Clue in the Dust              60
8   Kidnapped!                      69
9   A Narrow Escape                 80
10  Fire!                           89
11  Danger in Fashion               97
12  A Vandal at Large              106
13  Blues in the Night             116
14  The Puzzle Falls Together      125
15  The Island's Secret            137
16  Ablaze!                        145

# 1

## Set for Suspense

Nancy Drew paused at the curb, waiting for the light to change. A stiff breeze off nearby Lake Michigan whipped a few strands of her reddish blond hair across her face. Just a few blocks away, the skyscrapers of downtown Chicago gleamed in the morning light.

Nancy's friend Bess Marvin suddenly grabbed her arm. "Look, Nancy, there's Cindy!" she exclaimed. "There, on that billboard."

Nancy followed Bess's pointing finger. Across the street, mounted on the roof of a six-story brick building, was a big poster advertising a sale at a local department store. A tall, slim girl with honey blond hair was shown dashing happily across a street, carrying several shopping bags.

It was their friend Cindy Sunderland, a River Heights girl who had recently moved to Chicago to pursue a career in modeling. With its high cheekbones, tip-tilted nose, and dazzling sky blue eyes, Cindy's face was unmistakable. No wonder she was fast becoming one of the hottest teen models around.

"Isn't she terrific?" Bess added. "Just looking at her picture makes me want to go catch that sale."

Nancy laughed. "Come on, Bess," she said. "You've never seen a sale you didn't like."

Bess flushed. "Well, maybe you're right," she admitted. "But Cindy's picture does make that ad stand out. I just know she's going to be the next big supermodel. And it's so cool that she asked us to come watch her film this commercial— especially considering that we've only met her a few times."

Nancy giggled. "She could hardly *not* invite us, you dropped so many hints when we saw her last month," she reminded her friend. "But I think she wanted a little moral support, too. From what she said, it's a really big break in 'her career—to move up from ad photos and fashion shows to TV commercials. It could lead to an acting career someday. I bet she's pretty nervous."

Bess nodded. "It's too bad George had to go on a trip with her family this week. She would have loved to come along." George Fayne, Bess's cousin, was the third member of this trio of best friends.

The light changed. As they started across the street, Bess looked around at the run-down buildings. "Nancy, are you sure we're in the right place?" she asked nervously. She flinched as an elevated train rattled past the next intersection. "Nothing around here looks like a movie studio."

Nancy grinned. "This won't be that kind of studio, silly," she corrected Bess. "Cindy is making a commercial, not a feature film. Come on, the building must be on the next block."

The address Cindy had given them turned out to be that of a solid-looking brick building with wide-arched windows on the street level. Over the entrance a carved stone panel bore the name MacAllister's Stores. Elaborately sculpted vines and flowers wound through the old-fashioned lettering.

"Are you sure this is the place?" Bess asked, looking up at the stone panel.

"I have a hunch that MacAllister's went out of business a long time ago," Nancy replied. She pointed to a new brass plaque to the left of the entrance. "This is it, all right—The Chicago Film Center. We're supposed to go to the fourth floor, to Studio 4A."

The man at the information desk didn't even look up from his newspaper as they crossed the lobby. The elevator was an old-fashioned one, with a brass arrow above the door that pointed to the floor numbers. The elevator rumbled open, groaned when Nancy pressed Four, and started upward with a creak and a jerk.

"Next time let's take the stairs," Bess sug-

3

gested as something banged loudly against the outside of the elevator cab. "It'll probably be faster, and I *know* it'll be safer."

The elevator shuddered to a halt, and the door rattled open. The girls stepped out into the middle of a long, high-ceilinged hallway lit mostly by windows at either end. As they followed an arrow to the left, their footsteps echoed on the worn marble floors.

When they reached the metal double doors to Studio 4A, Nancy tried the knob. It was locked. Bess pressed the button on the intercom.

"Names?" a voice crackled through the speaker.

Nancy gave their names, and the door clicked open. Inside was a small, bare, white entry hall.

An unfriendly looking guy in his midtwenties came through the opposite doorway. His brown ponytail and the gold stud in his left earlobe screamed Fashion with a capital *F*. He wore tight jeans and a half-unbuttoned shirt with a designer logo embroidered on the pocket.

He held out his arms to block their way. "You are not on the approved list," he announced, hard-faced. "What do you want?"

"Cindy Sunderland invited us," Nancy explained.

"You're not on the list," the guy repeated. "This is a film studio, not a tourist attraction. Please do us a favor and go away."

"Now wait a minute," Bess said, raising her

voice. "We came all the way from River Heights because Cindy asked us to. Why don't you check with her if you don't believe us?"

Just then an older man with bushy steel gray hair appeared in the doorway. His faded T-shirt advertised a Mexican restaurant in Paris. "Is there a problem?" he asked, giving Nancy and Bess a warm smile. Laugh lines radiated from his twinkling blue eyes.

"I'm Nancy Drew," Nancy said, returning the smile. "And this is—"

"Ah yes," the man said, interrupting her. "Cindy told me about you. I believe you are a famous detective, Ms. Drew, no?" Hearing his slight accent, Nancy guessed he was from Italy.

Nancy smiled modestly. "I *have* solved a case or two," she admitted. "And this is my friend, Bess Marvin."

"I help Nancy out with her cases from time to time," Bess put in, trying to sound modest, too.

"Well, I'm very glad you could come," the man said, shaking their hands. "I am Carlo Festa, director and producer of Festa Films. I am supposed to be in charge of this madhouse." Carlo turned to the guy with the ponytail and added, "Why didn't you tell me they were here, Miklos?"

"I was sending them away," Miklos replied, holding up an open notebook. "They are not on the approved list."

Carlo snorted, took the notebook, and scribbled Bess and Nancy's names at the bottom of the page. "Now they are," he said. "In future, please consult me before you send away our guests. Is that clear?"

Miklos, red-faced, muttered, "Yes, Carlo." As he turned away, Nancy heard him add something under his breath. She didn't catch the words, but the resentful tone was all too clear.

"Come, I will show you what we are doing," Carlo said, taking Nancy and Bess by the arm. He led them toward an inner door.

As they stepped through the doorway, Nancy's eyes widened. The room they had entered was at least as big as a basketball court and jammed with people and equipment. Thick black cables snaked across the floor, held in place by strips of shiny silver tape. Nancy saw a man at the top of a tall stepladder, adjusting the big stage lights hanging from a grid just below the high ceiling.

Under the lights, one corner of the room had been set up to look like a sleek modern kitchen. A woman in a blue smock was carefully polishing the chrome handles of the cabinets.

A man in jeans, a purple sleeveless T-shirt, and a black leather vest hurried over. "Carlo?" he said. "That china pattern is a disaster! It makes the cereal look like a bowl of puppy chow!"

"It was Wei Lee's choice," Carlo replied in a calm voice. "She's the set decorator."

"And I'm the food stylist," the man retorted. "How can I make Healthibits look delicious in

6

the close-up shots if I'm forced to put it on ugly dishes?"

Carlo sighed. "All right, Stefan. How long will it take to change the plates?"

"No time at all," Stefan assured him. "I happened to bring some lovely china with me this morning. It'll be exactly right. It's from my personal collection, but I won't charge the client for using it."

He turned and walked back to the set before Carlo could reply. The director shrugged and looked over at Nancy and Bess. "In my next life, I want to be a lion tamer," he confided. "I am sure it is much easier on the nerves. Now, let me show you—"

He broke off as a woman in her forties strolled over. Nancy admired her elegant dark red dress and three strands of pearls.

"Ah, Stella," Carlo said. "Let me present Nancy Drew and Bess Marvin, friends from Cindy's hometown. Stella is from McVie and Martin, the advertising agency in charge of this campaign," he informed the girls.

"Hi there," Stella said, without even looking at Nancy and Bess. "Carlo, is everything set? You know how important it is to finish this on schedule. We're already running behind."

"I could not start until the script was written and approved," Carlo pointed out.

"No, of course not," Stella said, sighing. "I'm not complaining about you. But we've had such

7

problems every step of the way. It's almost as if this campaign is jinxed."

A man of about thirty, with gold-rimmed glasses and slicked-back hair, joined them in time to hear this. "Getting superstitious, Stella?" he joked, with an odd, sneering smile. "Why don't you let my team at the agency handle this one? You could even go off on a little vacation. You could certainly use one."

Stella's nostrils flared. "I'm very grateful for your help, Erik," she said. "But I'm quite capable of supervising the campaign myself." Nancy exchanged a glance with Bess. She saw that her friend, too, had picked up on the tensions gathering in the studio.

Carlo put one hand on Stella's shoulder and the other on Erik's. "Erik, meet Nancy and Bess. Erik is also from McVie and Martin," he explained. Then he added soothingly, "I want us all to have fun and make a wonderful commercial. There are just one or two details about the script I need to discuss. Girls, will you excuse me for a moment? I'll ask my assistant, Charmaine, to show you around."

He glanced around the busy studio. Just then a young woman with her black hair braided in cornrows came striding over. The dozen silver bracelets on her left forearm jingled as she walked.

"Ah, Charmaine," Carlo said, smiling. "I was just looking for you. Could you—"

"We've got a problem," Charmaine interrupted him. "It's Cindy."

"The makeup artist is not done with her yet?" Carlo asked. "Don't worry. We have the lighting and sound checks to do before we need her."

"It's not that, Carlo," Charmaine replied. "Cindy isn't here yet."

Carlo stared at her, then looked at his watch. "Impossible!" he exploded. "She knew she was to be here by eight-thirty, and now it is almost ten! Is *this* what people in the business mean when they tell me she's reliable?"

Then he paused and took a deep breath. "Call her apartment," he suggested, calming himself down. "Perhaps she overslept. Tell her we'll have a car at her door in ten minutes."

Charmaine tugged nervously at one of her big hoop earrings. "I did call," she said. "I spoke to Ann Bowers, her agent. Cindy lives with her, you know. Ms. Bowers said Cindy was already gone when she got up this morning."

The assistant drew a trembling breath. "She thought Cindy must have come straight here, skipping her morning run and everything," she went on. "But now she's afraid that something may have happened to Cindy . . . something terrible!"

# 2

# *Missing!*

Nancy looked at Bess in alarm. Cindy, missing? Right at the start of such a big assignment? This could ruin her career!

"Maybe Bess and I can help find her," Nancy said to Carlo.

"No, no, no," Carlo said. He smiled, but he couldn't hide the worry in his eyes. "It is nice of you to offer. But I am sure she made a mistake about the time, that's all."

"I spoke to Cindy yesterday afternoon," Charmaine said. "She said she'd see me at eight-thirty sharp. She even asked if she could come earlier, but I told her not to bother—no one would be ready for her."

"Could she have been in an accident?" Bess wondered.

Charmaine replied, "Cindy doesn't have a car. She would probably have taken a taxi here. Ms. Bowers said she was going to call the police and the hospitals. I don't know what else we can do. We can't exactly go out and search the whole city of Chicago."

"This is a big fuss about very little," Carlo insisted. "I am sure Cindy will be here any moment. But I must announce the delay."

He turned, cupped his hands around his mouth, and said loudly, "Your attention, people! We are making a small change in the schedule. Everything is pushed back two hours. Thank you."

A buzz of conversation filled the big room. A young woman with incredibly short black hair hurried over. She was wearing a clean white smock.

"Ah, Ghalia," Carlo said, taking her arm. To Nancy and Bess, he added, "Ghalia is one of the best makeup artists in Chicago. We are very lucky to have her on our team."

"Thanks, Carlo," Ghalia said, with a quick smile. "But I've got a conflict. You see, I'm due at another session at noon."

Carlo squeezed her shoulder. "Don't worry," he said. "We will have you out in plenty of time."

"I know Cindy," Ghalia persisted. "I've made her up for two or three fashion shoots. I'll need forty-five minutes to do a good job on her. All those angles that make her face so beautiful make my job tough."

Carlo rolled his eyes. "I know all this, Ghalia," he said patiently. "I am not new to this business,

11

you know. You will have the time you need, or else we will postpone the shoot."

A balding man in a dark suit came up in time to hear Carlo's last words. "Postpone the shoot?" he said, his voice rising. "Carlo, you can't! This campaign's on a very tight schedule—and a tight budget, too. We've got no room for cost over-runs."

The man reached inside his jacket toward his shirt pocket. As he did, Nancy noticed yellow stains on his first two fingers. She wasn't surprised to see him pull out a pack of cigarettes.

"Sorry, Mr. Pike," Charmaine said quickly. "No smoking in the studio. You can go upstairs to the office, if you like. It's empty."

"Ridiculous," Pike muttered, as he slid the cigarettes back in his pocket. "Anyway, listen, Carlo. Do you realize how much our company has riding on Healthibits?"

Stella stepped forward and said to Pike, "Sherman, I'm delighted that you could come down to watch this morning. But you put this ad campaign in the hands of our agency. Don't you think you ought to let us do our job?"

"Oh—sorry, Stella," Pike said. "But you know how much this campaign means to us . . . and to me, personally. I can't help feeling involved."

Carlo looked around at the crowd gathering to listen. He frowned. "Stella, Erik, Sherman—I think we should all go upstairs to my office. We can talk more comfortably there." He started

12

away, then looked over his shoulder and added, "Charmaine, please look after Bess and Nancy. Show them around and explain what is happening."

The crowd broke up. Charmaine smiled at Nancy and Bess. "It's not always this crazy around here," she confided.

"What do you think happened to Cindy?" Bess asked.

Charmaine shook her head. "I don't know," she replied. "To tell the truth, I'm worried. Cindy and I, we're pretty tight, and I know how excited she was about this job. She wouldn't just not show up. Anyone in the business will tell you how reliable and hardworking she is, even people who may think she has weird ideas."

Nancy instantly caught the hint of something odd in Charmaine's words. "Weird ideas?" she repeated.

Charmaine hesitated. "I'm not saying *I* think they're weird, but . . . well, not long ago Cindy was booked for an ad for a big cosmetics company. Then she found out that they test their products on animals. She thinks animal testing is cruel, so she turned down the job. Ms. Bowers was furious about it, but Cindy wouldn't give in."

Nancy nodded, taking in the information. "You mentioned Ms. Bowers before," she said. "Who's she?"

"Ann Bowers?" Charmaine replied. "Oh, I forgot you guys aren't in the business. If you

13

were, you'd definitely know her name. She's the head of one of the most important modeling agencies in the Midwest. Signing with her was Cindy's first big break. Ann Bowers can open all kinds of doors for a model. And she really believes in taking care of her 'girls.' That's why Cindy's mom was so pleased when Ms. Bowers offered to let Cindy stay at her apartment."

"You mean Cindy shares an apartment with her boss?" Bess asked, puzzled.

Charmaine laughed. "Not really. Ms. Bowers is more like her housemother," she said. "She's always got two or three of her teen models living with her. It makes their parents feel better about their kids living in the big city. She's got this huge apartment over on Lake Shore Drive. It must have ten or twelve rooms. Cindy has her own bedroom, and so does her friend Gayle. Gayle's with the Bowers Agency, too."

Nancy made a mental note to talk to Ann Bowers as soon as possible. She would probably know as much about Cindy's activities as anyone.

"Do you have *any* idea why Cindy didn't show up this morning?" Nancy asked Charmaine.

Charmaine shook her head. "I wish I did," she said with a sigh. "I know she's had some problems lately, but I can't believe she'd blow something as important as this."

Bess glanced at Nancy, then asked, "Problems? What kind of problems?"

Charmaine made a face. "Oh, just boyfriend

problems," she answered. "She's been seeing this guy, Cody Charles. He's in law school. He's an okay guy, I guess, except that he's kind of down on her modeling career. I don't know why—she's got a fantastic future. Maybe he's a little bit jealous of her success."

"He wouldn't abduct her just because he doesn't like her career," Nancy pointed out. "Still, he may have some idea of what happened to her. Do you know his phone number?"

"I think Cindy gave it to me once." Charmaine leafed through her address book. "Yeah, here." She scribbled the number on a scrap of paper, then led Nancy to the phone.

Cody answered on the second ring. When Nancy explained why she was calling, he immediately sounded alarmed. "Let me get this straight," he said. "Cindy didn't show up at the studio this morning? And Ms. Bowers doesn't know where she is?"

"That's right," Nancy replied. "Do you—"

Cody interrupted her. "We were planning to get together this evening," he said, sounding a little hysterical. "If you do track her down, tell her to call me right away, okay? I'm studying for an exam, but I'll try to make a few calls myself. Thanks for letting me know." There was a click, followed by silence.

Nancy held the receiver away from her face and stared at it, trying to picture the guy who had just hung up on her. Cody Charles seemed more concerned about whether Cindy would make their date than about the fact that she hadn't shown up for work. That was kind of odd.

Hanging up, Nancy turned to look for Bess and Charmaine. She nearly bumped into Miklos, the ponytailed guy who had met her and Bess so rudely at the door. He scowled at her and slouched away.

Nancy watched him go uneasily. He'd been standing awfully close behind her. Had he been eavesdropping on her phone call? And if so, why?

Rejoining Bess and Charmaine, Nancy briefly told them what she'd learned from Cody. "He wasn't much help," she added dryly.

"This is a disaster," Charmaine fretted. "Carlo only reserved this studio for four days. If we lose a whole day's shooting time, we could be in a real crunch."

Bess gave her a puzzled look. "Isn't this Carlo's studio?" she asked.

Charmaine laughed. "No way! Do you know what a place like this costs? This building used to be a department store, but it went out of business years ago. It stood empty for ages until the city helped convert it to a film center. Lots of small production companies like ours have offices here.

"Whenever we need to, we rent one of the soundstages," she continued. "But they're usually booked well in advance. If we need more time, we have to find some other company who'll sell us their time slot. Or else we have to move the whole shoot to another studio somewhere. And that would cost Carlo a mint."

So this delay was really hurting Carlo, too, Nancy mused. Could someone have detained Cindy to hurt Carlo's business? She was just about to ask Charmaine if Carlo had any enemies, when the director called from the doorway.

"Charmaine? Could you please come to the office?" he asked. "We have some arranging to do."

Charmaine said goodbye to the girls and followed him off the soundstage.

"Nancy?" Bess said. "Shouldn't we try to find Cindy? She might be in some kind of trouble."

"I agree, but I need to ask Carlo and Charmaine a few more questions first," Nancy replied. "I wonder where Carlo's office is."

Bess glanced around. "There's Stella, over by the set," she said. "We can ask her."

Nancy and Bess started across the soundstage. Then suddenly Nancy halted, touching Bess's arm and signaling her to be silent. Stella was in the middle of a heated argument with someone hidden by the edge of the set's wall.

"—not to interfere," Stella was saying in a steely voice. "*I'm* in charge of this account. You're here as an observer."

"*And* advisor." Nancy recognized Erik's voice. "And here's my advice. Cindy Sunderland's contract has an escape clause. Anytime she misses an engagement without a valid reason, we can can-

cel her contract. Well, she's just missed one—
let's get rid of her."

Nancy and Bess exchanged worried looks.

"I know all that," Stella replied. "But what if
she *does* have a valid reason?"

Erik snorted. "I'm sorry, Stella, but the girl's a
total flake," he declared. "I've said so all along.
We should dump her before we've invested any
more in her. We can't let her take this whole
campaign down the tubes."

"Look, Erik," Stella said patiently. "I chose
Cindy over a couple of dozen other candidates,
because she has exactly the looks and personality
we want. I'm not going to throw all that away, just
because she's an hour or so late."

Nancy was listening intently. Suddenly, out of
the corner of her eye, she sensed something
moving. She looked up and froze.

To the right of Erik and Stella, the wall of the
set was tilting dangerously forward—and still
falling. They were turned away from it, so they
hadn't noticed, but they were right in its path. At
any second it was going to crash down on them!

# 3

# Sabotage?

"Look out!" Nancy shouted. The wall of the set toppled forward with increasing speed. Stella and Erik turned around. Panic filled their eyes as they saw the danger they were in.

Nancy dashed forward, but before she could reach them Erik had yanked Stella aside. An instant later the set wall crashed to the floor, sending up a thick cloud of dust. There were shouts of alarm from around the studio. People came running.

Carlo came running back into the studio and shoved through the crowd to reach Stella and Erik. "What happened? Are you all right?" he demanded.

Before they could answer, Stefan, the food stylist, fell to his knees and scrabbled around in the debris. "Oh, no!" he cried, clapping his hand to his forehead. "My china! Carlo, I hope you're well insured. That was genuine Depression ware—it's irreplaceable!"

"We can talk about that later, Stefan," Carlo replied. "For now, I am more concerned to know how the set could collapse like this."

Nancy had been wondering the same thing. She had already moved around to the back of the set to study the way it was put together. The walls—frames of two-by-fours covered with wallboard—were held upright by triangular wooden struts that braced the walls against the floor. Heavy canvas sandbags were draped over the bottom of each strut, to hold it in place.

There were sandbags along the line where the fallen wall had stood, too. But they lay in a neat line on the floor, apparently undisturbed. Either they had never been put properly in place, or someone had moved them off the supports. The set wall had been so precariously balanced that almost anything—a draft of air, vibrations from a passing train—might make it fall over. And something obviously had.

Carlo came over and stared down at the sandbags, then met Nancy's eyes. His jaw tightened in anger.

"Miklos!" he shouted. "Where is Miklos?"

The guy with the ponytail appeared from behind the far end of the set. Nancy wondered what he'd been doing there. Why hadn't he come running when the set wall fell, the way everyone else had?

"Here I am," he said sullenly. "What's the problem?"

Carlo gestured at the fallen wall. "Problem?" he repeated. "Problem? I put you in charge of checking over the set. You didn't do it."

"I did so!" Miklos insisted. "I was the first one here this morning. I looked at everything. It was just as it should be."

Nancy stepped forward. "Those sandbags," she said, pointing to the bottom of the struts. "Were they weighing down the set supports?"

Miklos glared at her. "Of course. That's what they're there for, to keep the set from falling over," he replied in a testy voice.

"But the set *did* fall over," Nancy reminded him. "And the sandbags are still sitting on the floor in a little line."

"Then somebody must have moved them," Miklos said with a shrug. "They were in place this morning. That's all I know."

"That's not good enough," Carlo said. "I have given you more than one warning. I told you what would happen the next time there was a problem. Now I have finally had it. You're fired, Miklos. Come back at the end of the day and I will pay you what you are owed."

"You can't—" Miklos started to say. Then he stopped. Turning on his heel, he stomped toward the door. He gave Nancy a dirty look as he passed her.

Carlos clapped his hands together loudly.

"People?" he called out. "Enough gaping. Let's get this set back in order, okay?" With a buzz of excited gossiping, the crew moved into action.

"Whew!" Bess murmured, appearing at Nancy's side. "I think we just lost our places on Miklos's list of favorite people."

"I can live with that," Nancy said dryly. "What I'm wondering is—did he really sabotage the set? He had plenty of chances."

"But why would he do that?" Bess demanded.

Nancy shrugged. "I don't know," she admitted. "But he sure has an attitude about something. Maybe Carlo can tell us."

They found Carlo watching as three of the crew members put the set back together. "Get Wei Lee on the phone," he was telling Charmaine. "Tell her we need her here right away. I think the set will need only some touch-up paint—at least, I hope so."

As Charmaine headed for the telephone, Nancy stepped over to Carlo, with Bess right behind her. "Carlo, about this incident," Nancy said quietly. "Can you think of anybody who might want to delay your work? Miklos, for example?"

Carlo gave her a shrewd glance. "I was wondering the same myself," he replied. "First, Cindy does not arrive. Now this accident to the set. I hope it was simple carelessness on the part of Miklos, but I do not know. Could someone hate me so much?"

"It might not be personal," Bess pointed out. "What if a business rival just wanted to hurt your reputation?"

Carlo shook his head wearily. "You may be right. What a world it is!" he said. "Nancy, you and Bess offered to help before, to look for Cindy. I said no then. Is your offer still open?"

Nancy glanced at Bess, who met her eyes in eager agreement. "You bet," Nancy told Carlo.

The director beamed with relief. "Wonderful!" he exclaimed. "If only you can find out who is causing these problems, then everything will be fine."

"We'll get right on it," Nancy promised him.

As the lighting director broke in to ask Carlo a few questions, Nancy took Bess aside. "Let's get Ann Bowers's phone number from Charmaine," she suggested. "If we can trace Cindy's movements this morning, maybe it'll give us an idea of what might have happened to her."

Over the phone, Ann Bowers agreed to see Bess and Nancy. On Charmaine's advice, they took a cab to the address on Lake Shore Drive. They pulled up in front of a luxury apartment tower facing a green park. The doorman directed them to the seventeenth floor, to apartment 17M.

The door to 17M was right across from the elevator. Before Nancy could buzz, it swung open.

A woman with carefully styled bright blond

hair greeted them. Nancy guessed her to be about forty. "You must be Nancy and Bess," she said. "I'm Ann Bowers. Please come in."

As Ms. Bowers led them into the living room, Nancy heard Bess let out a tiny gulp of admiration. The room was large, with gilt-framed paintings, pale carpeting, and elegant striped silk wallpaper. The far wall was all windows, with an amazing view across the park to Lake Michigan.

Ms. Bowers motioned them to a pale leather sofa, then pulled a flowered brocade armchair around to face them. As she sat, she smoothed down her chic sky blue dress and posed her slender legs neatly to the side. "I'm so pleased to meet you," she said. "Cindy has told me all about you. Your visit may be the only bright spot in this whole terrible morning."

Nancy decided to dive right in. "Ms. Bowers, do you have any idea why Cindy didn't show up at the studio this morning?"

"None whatsoever," Ms. Bowers replied. She fiddled with a pair of gold-rimmed reading glasses dangling from a chain of turquoise beads around her neck. "Frankly, I'm worried. This assignment is a huge step up for Cindy. Not many models make the jump to commercials. And hardly anyone this young has the opportunity to be a spokesperson for a major new product."

"Spokesperson?" Bess said. "I thought she was just appearing in a commercial."

"Not just one commercial," Ms. Bowers

corrected her. "Cindy is contracted for four commercials, with an option to continue for four more. And she'll be making personal appearances all around the country—at sports events, outdoor festivals, anything that's likely to attract teens. Healthibits, you see, is a new cereal designed for young people who care about nutrition but still want good taste."

Nancy hid a smile. Ms. Bowers was sounding like a Healthibits spokesperson herself. "When was the last time you saw Cindy?" she asked.

"Why, early yesterday evening," Ms. Bowers replied, frowning as she tried to remember. "I had to go to the theater with some colleagues, but I made a point of chatting with Cindy before I left. I urged her to get a good night's sleep. These girls think nothing of watching television until all hours the night before a shoot!"

"What sort of mood was she in?" Bess asked.

Ms. Bowers hesitated. "Excited, I'd say, and naturally a bit nervous," she answered.

"Was there anything unusual in the way she was acting?" asked Nancy.

"Not in the least," Ms. Bowers insisted. "And I don't care much for this line of questioning. You surely can't think Cindy missed this assignment on purpose! She is a total professional. She has never missed an engagement, not even a minor go-see."

Bess blinked. "What's that?" she asked.

Ms. Bowers smiled. "Sorry. That's when a

model is sent to a photographer or agency that's looking for someone. We say, 'Go see so-and-so,' so it's called a go-see."

Nancy pressed on. "So you didn't speak to Cindy when you got home from the theater?"

"No, she was already asleep," Bowers replied.

"Did you look in on her?" Bess asked.

Ms. Bowers looked offended. "Certainly not," she said. "Her door was closed. I have the greatest respect for my girls' privacy."

"Then you don't actually know that she was here," Nancy pointed out. "Think carefully. This could be important."

"I see that," Ms. Bowers said. "Well, I didn't actually see her in bed, but when I went to the kitchen for a glass of milk, I noticed a glass and bowl in the dish rack, still wet. Cindy believes in letting dishes air-dry." Ms. Bowers rolled her eyes. "It's one of her little quirks."

Nancy worked through her thoughts out loud. "So she apparently had a snack at about—what time did you get home?"

"Shortly after eleven," Ms. Bowers replied.

"And Cindy was already gone when you got up this morning?" Bess asked.

Ms. Bowers nodded. "That's right. The door to her room was open, and the bed was made," she said. "Cindy likes to get up early and go for a run along the lake, so I assumed that that was what she had done. When she didn't come back, I assumed she'd gone straight to the studio. The first hint I had that anything was wrong was when Charmaine called.

"I immediately called the police and the local hospitals," Ms. Bowers went on, sounding more upset. "But they had no news of her. I called her mother in River Heights, but she hadn't heard from Cindy, either. Do you think—"

She broke off at the sound of a key in the door lock. Bess and Nancy looked around.

For a moment Nancy thought it was Cindy coming home. The girl in the doorway was tall and slim, like Cindy, and had shoulder-length hair of almost the same honey blond color. But up close, Nancy saw that this girl's face was quite different—narrower and sharper.

When she saw Nancy and Bess, the girl halted and frowned. "Come in, Gayle," Ms. Bowers called. "Come meet Cindy's friends. Is that Jason there with you?"

Gayle strolled into the living room, followed by a broad-shouldered guy with short-cut sandy hair. He tossed three shopping bags from Michigan Avenue department stores onto a nearby chair.

Nancy glanced over at Bess and caught a flash of envy on her face. It must be nice to be able to go on such a shopping spree—and even have a hunk to carry your packages home for you!

27

Ms. Bowers introduced Nancy and Bess, then gravely told Gayle and Jason about Cindy.

Gayle's eyes widened. "Really?" she said. "That's awful!" She stared at the floor, dumbstruck, for a moment. Then she looked up, swallowing hard. "What could have made her run away from such a wonderful opportunity?" she asked.

"There's no reason to think she *did* run away," Ms. Bowers pointed out.

Nancy was intrigued by Gayle's reaction. "Why did you assume Cindy ran away?" she asked.

Gayle looked over at her boyfriend, then back at Nancy. With a troubled expression, she said, "Maybe I shouldn't mention this, but I guess I was half expecting something like this."

Ms. Bowers's face stiffened. "How can you say such a thing?" she demanded.

"Cindy was doing her best not to let you see it," Gayle said slowly. "But she was starting to have second thoughts about this new gig. For one thing, she'd have to be on the road for months and months—away from Cody. She didn't think she'd like that."

"When did she tell you this?" Nancy asked.

"Last night," Gayle replied. "Jason and I were on our way out to a movie. Just before we left, Cindy took me aside and told me that she wanted to give up the Healthibits campaign, but she was too scared to say so to Ms. Bowers.

"She was talking a little wildly," Gayle went on. "She said the only way she could get out of it would be to vanish. I bet that's exactly what she did!"

# 4

## Runaway Model

Nancy stared at Gayle. Had Cindy really threatened to run away? It seemed so unlike the girl Nancy knew, but then how well did she really know her, after all?

"Did Cindy say anything about where she might go?" Nancy asked.

Before Gayle could respond, Ms. Bowers broke in, "Really, Gayle, I'm astonished at you. Spreading such a rumor about your best friend! You know very well how pleased Cindy was when she won the Healthibits job. And you know how much she was looking forward to the filming this morning."

A stubborn look settled on Gayle's face as she plopped down on a leather footstool. "I'm telling you the truth," she declared.

"That's right," Jason added. "Cindy was really nervous. She said she wished Gayle had got the

Healthibits assignment instead. You know that Gayle was up for it, too."

"Of course I believe you, Gayle," Ms. Bowers said soothingly, "but consider the circumstances. It was the night before an important new job—naturally Cindy was nervous. Anyone would be. And maybe she did make some wild statements about running away. But saying it and doing it are very different things. Cindy would never throw away her big break because of an attack of nerves."

"If you say so, Ann," Gayle replied. As she turned away, Nancy saw her expression. It was boiling with resentment and rebellion.

Ms. Bowers must have seen it, too. "Wait a moment, dear," she continued. "I know you're just trying to be helpful. You've always been so supportive of Cindy—not like some people."

Bess jumped in. "What do you mean by that, Ms. Bowers?" she asked.

The older woman hesitated. "I detest spreading gossip," she finally said. "But I've seen for myself that Cindy's friend Cody has been less than helpful in many ways."

"I hear that he wants Cindy to give up the Healthibits campaign," Nancy said. "Is that true?"

"I gather he's unhappy that Cindy will have to travel a great deal," Ms. Bowers replied. She turned in her chair and began rearranging the

31

flowers in a vase on the side table. With her back to Nancy and Bess, she added, "I can't believe he'd stand in the way of Cindy's success, though. And I find it just as hard to believe that Cindy would listen to such bad advice."

"What *do* you think happened to her?" Bess asked. "I mean, face it. She didn't show up at the studio this morning. Something happened."

Ms. Bowers paused, still facing away. "As I said earlier to Carlo Festa's assistant," she finally said, "I have a—a feeling that something terrible has happened. I hope I'm wrong, but I'm very frightened for Cindy's safety."

Gayle leaned toward the modeling agent and laid a hand on her arm. "Please don't worry, Ann," she urged. "I'm sure Cindy's okay. She probably just needed to get away and think things over."

"I hope you're right," Ms. Bowers said. "And if you are, I hope Stella Laporte will overlook this morning's absence. It would be a disaster if she invoked the escape clause in Cindy's contract."

From somewhere in the room, a telephone chirped. "Excuse me," Ms. Bowers said. "I'm expecting a call from Paris." She rose and crossed to an antique Chinese lacquer cabinet, opening it to take out a cordless phone. "Jean-Pierre? *Salut! Comment ça va?*" she spoke into it.

While Ms. Bowers continued in rapid-fire French, Nancy asked Gayle, "Did you see Cindy at all today?"

Gayle shook her head. "No. Her door was shut when I left, at around eight-thirty. I don't know if she was still asleep or if she'd already gone out."

"Were you modeling this morning?" Bess asked.

"No, I had the morning free," Gayle told her. "So I talked Jason into taking time off and meeting me for breakfast and some shopping. He's working part-time in his uncle's shipping company while he goes to business school."

"Which reminds me, I'd better put in some library time," Jason said. He came over and gave Gayle a peck on the cheek. "Call you later."

He left. A moment later Ms. Bowers finished her call. "Well!" she said, beaming as she turned back to the girls. "Jean-Pierre is going to be in town next month to open a boutique at one of the big department stores. It's sure to get nationwide TV and press coverage. And guess what agency he's asking to supply *all* the models!"

"Ann, that's glorious!" Gayle said, running over and giving her a hug. "I can hardly wait!"

"Congratulations, Ms. Bowers," Nancy said politely. "That's really exciting." She paused, then added, "I wonder—would you mind if Bess and I take a look at Cindy's room? We might find some clue to what happened to her."

Ms. Bowers's face sobered. "Yes, of course," she replied. "It's just down the hall, the first door on the left. Please call if I can help you in any way."

After locating the room, Nancy and Bess opened Cindy's door and paused to look around. Like the living room, the bedroom had thick carpeting and wide windows overlooking the lake.

"Wow, fabulous!" Bess commented. "I'd love to have that Bruce Springsteen poster."

Nancy smiled. Cindy had hung the picture of the high-energy rock star right next to a huge poster for a movie of Sleeping Beauty. It looked like the Boss was trying to wake up the fairy-tale princess, with no luck. Over the bed, a shelf full of stuffed animals watched placidly. The other furnishings included a low white dresser, a wicker chair with a flowered cushion, and an old-fashioned dressing table topped by a big triple mirror. A stereo sat on the floor near the chair, with CDs and cassettes scattered around it.

To Nancy, the room spoke of someone who enjoyed surrounding herself with nice things and who could afford to do it. That didn't match very well with the picture Gayle had painted of a nervous, depressed runaway.

Nancy nodded to a closet door in the corner. "Let's see if Cindy's running outfit is gone," she suggested. "At least that would tell us that she disappeared during her morning run."

She pulled the door open, revealing a walk-in closet jammed with clothes. On the floor were a dozen or more pairs of shoes, from brightly colored suede flats to high-tech cross-trainers.

Looking over Nancy's shoulder, Bess sighed longingly at the sight of all those clothes. "I see three or four running suits hanging up," she said. "And she could've been wearing still another one."

Nancy nodded. "It's no use trying to have Gayle or Ms. Bowers figure out what Cindy might be wearing," she said. "She's got so much stuff here, even *she* probably couldn't tell what was missing."

"Free samples from trendy designers, I bet," Bess said enviously as she turned away from the closet. "Hey, speaking of samples, this must be the cereal Cindy's going to be advertising."

Bess picked up a plain white box labeled Sample—Not for Public Distribution or Resale. The top flap was open. Bess shook some of the contents into her hand. Nancy thought that it looked like granola.

Bess popped the handful into her mouth. "Hey, not bad," she decided. "Not bad at all."

Nancy grinned. "As soon as you're done with snack time, can we go on with our search?"

Bess blushed. "Sorry," she said. Taking one more handful, she put the cereal box down and began going through the drawers of the dresser.

Nancy spent a few more minutes on the closet, then checked out the small adjoining bathroom. In the shower stall, she saw several small bottles of shampoos, most of them brands she'd never heard of. The cabinet over the sink was filled with natural cold remedies and allergy medicines.

Nancy read the labels on a few of the containers. Did Cindy have real health problems, or was she one of those people who took something every time they had a sniffle? she wondered.

After a further look around, she returned to the bedroom. "Find anything?" she asked Bess.

"Not really," Bess replied. "You?"

Nancy made a face. "No," she answered. "Let's see if we can get Cindy's boyfriend to tell us anything. He must know *something* that would help."

Finding Ms. Bowers in her home office, they asked to use her phone there. Nancy dialed the number Charmaine had given her for Cody. After three rings, she heard an unusual buzz. A moment later, an oddly echoing voice said, "Hello?"

"Hello, is that Cody? This is Nancy Drew," she responded.

"Oh, good, I've been trying to reach you," Cody said. "No one at Festa's place seemed to know where you'd gone. I had my calls forwarded to my car phone, so I wouldn't miss you. Listen, I need to talk to you. Can we get together?"

"You have some news about Cindy?" Nancy asked eagerly. Cody seemed much more willing to cooperate now than he had earlier.

"I'll tell you when I see you," he said. "I'm on my way back from Evanston now. Let's meet on the steps of the Art Institute in half an hour. Just so you'll recognize me, I've got black hair and I'm wearing a red sweater."

Nancy checked her watch and said, "Okay, my friend Bess and I will be there."

On the way out, Nancy questioned the doorman. He knew Cindy well, but he hadn't seen her leave the building that morning. "She could have gone out through the garage, though," he said. "You girls want a cab?"

The Art Institute was a sprawling museum set in a park near the lake. Nancy and Bess arrived right on time and waited near one of the two large bronze lions flanking the wide steps.

"I don't see anyone in a red sweater," Nancy said, scanning the steps and the sidewalk.

"I do," Bess replied. "Across the street, waiting for the light—see him? Wow, look at those shoulders. He must work out a lot."

When the light changed, the guy in the red sweater crossed the street with an easy stride. He had the build of a running back, with broad shoulders and narrow hips. He had a square-jawed face and thick black hair. Spotting Bess and Nancy, he waved and jogged over to them.

"Bess and Nancy?" he asked as he reached them. "Sorry I'm late. Parking is murder here in the Loop. How about a cup of coffee or something? I know a quiet place nearby where we can talk."

Cody led them around the corner to a small

self-service sandwich bar. They bought coffees at the counter and sat down at a round marble-topped table. Nancy immediately asked, "What about Cindy? Have you found out anything?"

Cody shook his head. Looking down at the table, he said, "It's a total mystery. Cindy told me that you're a detective, Nancy. I hope you can solve this one."

Nancy gave him a puzzled look. Why had he asked for this meeting, if he didn't have anything new to tell them?

"We hear that you didn't want Cindy to take this Healthibits job," Bess said bluntly. "Do you think she decided to take your advice?"

Cody gave Bess a narrow glance. "Who told you that—Ann Bowers?" he demanded. "That's stupid. Okay, I'm not thrilled that Cindy will have to be away so much. But I know it's a terrific chance for her, and she's really looking forward to it. She wouldn't mess it up, and I wouldn't, either."

"Then why didn't she show up at the studio this morning?" Nancy asked.

Cody spread his hands wide. "That's the question, isn't it? I don't know," he admitted.

"When did you see Cindy last?" asked Bess.

"Last night," he replied. "We met for pizza, then I dropped her at home about eight. I wanted to see a movie, too, but she said she wanted to get lots of rest before this morning."

He paused, as if trying to make up his mind

about something. Then, speaking so low that Nancy had to lean closer to hear him, he said: "I'm worried sick. Something's happened to Cindy, I'm sure of it. An accident, maybe, or . . ."

Cody swallowed unhappily and went on, "I don't even want to think about it, but—I'm terrified that somebody's kidnapped her!"

# 5

## Friends and Enemies

"Kidnapped!" Bess echoed.

Cody met her eyes and nodded solemnly.

"Why do you say that?" Nancy asked. "Do you have any evidence?"

"No," Cody admitted. "Not a bit. But I can't imagine what else could have kept her from the studio, today of all days."

"Why would someone kidnap Cindy?" Bess asked, puzzled. "Her family isn't rich. I mean, they're not the kind of people who could pay a big ransom to get her released."

Cody frowned. "No, that's true, but Cindy's at the start of what could be a very big career," he pointed out. "What if the kidnappers think she's made a lot more money than she really has? Or what if they hope the Healthibits people would pay a big ransom to get her back?"

"That doesn't make sense," Nancy said. "Cindy isn't known yet as the Healthibits spokes-

40

person. Why would anyone think the company would pay to get her back at this point in the campaign? It would be a lot easier for them just to get someone else to take her place."

Cody's jaw dropped. "Then that must be it!" he exclaimed. "Somebody is trying to destroy Cindy's career!"

"Can you think of anyone who hates her enough to do that?" Nancy asked. "She certainly never struck me as the kind of person who makes a lot of enemies."

Cody hesitated. "I don't want to accuse anybody," he said finally. "But I'll tell you this much. Cindy hasn't been totally happy with the way Ann Bowers handled her deal with the Healthibits people. I looked over the contract later, and if you ask me, the terms are pretty one-sided. They can send her anywhere at any time, and if she refuses to go, she loses the whole job. When I pointed that out to Cindy, she was pretty annoyed. She started thinking about finding a new agent."

"Why wouldn't Ms. Bowers support Cindy?" Nancy asked. "I assume Ms. Bowers gets a percentage of the money. That alone should make her want the best deal for Cindy."

Cody shrugged, toying with his coffee spoon. "I don't know, but Cindy tried to talk to Ms. Bowers about it, and she didn't get anywhere. Bowers even hinted that Cindy could be replaced by someone who was more cooperative."

"You mean like Gayle, or one of the other teen models whom Bowers represents?" Bess asked shrewdly.

"I didn't say that," Cody replied quickly.

"But Cindy is already successful," Nancy pointed out. "And well on her way to being a lot more successful. Why would her own agent want to ruin her career?"

"I'm not saying she does," Cody said. He was starting to look as though he regretted having said anything at all. "I'm just thinking out loud, that's all."

Nancy looked carefully at Cody. "It's funny that you think Ann Bowers might be have something to do with Cindy's disappearance," she said offhandedly. "Because Bowers thinks *you* might be behind it."

Cody sat up in alarm. "Me? That's the most ridiculous thing I've ever heard!" he protested. "Why would I kidnap Cindy?"

Nancy was about to point out that no one had accused him of kidnapping her, only of being involved in her disappearance. But before she could, Cody pushed his chair back and stood up.

"Look, I can't just sit here chatting," he said brusquely. "Cindy's in some kind of trouble and she needs me."

"We're trying to help, too," Nancy told him, getting to her feet.

Cody looked away. "I know that, and I'm grateful for anything you can do," he muttered.

42

"Look, forget what I just said, okay? Knowing that Cindy may be in danger has me totally stressed out. I don't really think Ann Bowers had her kidnapped. The truth is, I don't know what to think. I'm sorry."

Jamming his hands deep in his pants pockets, Cody strode out of the sandwich bar. Nancy and Bess followed him out onto the sidewalk. "How can we get in touch with you if we need to?" Nancy asked.

"Just phone me," Cody told her. "If I'm not home, the calls are automatically forwarded to my car. I work part-time for a real estate agent in my hometown, and he installed the phone so that he can always reach me. Please, call me the minute you have any news about Cindy. And if I find out something, where will you be?"

"The rest of today, you can reach us at Carlo's office," Nancy replied. "If we're not there, just leave word and we'll call you as soon as we can. Tonight we'll be going back to River Heights. I'll give you my number there." She scribbled it on a scrap of paper and handed it to him.

Cody went off to retrieve his car. Nancy and Bess decided to walk back to Carlo's studio. Luckily, they'd planned to spend the whole day in Chicago, though they certainly couldn't have predicted they'd spend it this way.

"I'm really wondering whom we can trust," Nancy confided to Bess as they walked. "As far as we know at this point, Cindy had no reason to miss the session this morning, and every reason to be there. That makes it look as if someone prevented her. But who, and why?"

"We have lots of suspects," Bess said.

"Too many," Nancy replied. "Everybody seems to want to cast suspicion on everybody else. And frankly, so far I haven't heard a decent motive for any of them. Take Ms. Bowers's theory that Cody did it. Can you imagine him abducting Cindy just to keep her from taking a job? She wouldn't stay his girlfriend for a minute if he pulled a stunt like that. Ridiculous!"

"But what if he got someone else to do it, someone Cindy doesn't know?" Bess suggested. "They'd only have to keep her out of sight long enough to make the ad agency fire her."

Nancy looked skeptical. "Kidnapping's a federal offense, Bess," she pointed out. "Would a guy like Cody run the risk of having the FBI after him, just to keep his girlfriend from taking a few trips away from Chicago?"

"I guess not," Bess admitted. "But what if somebody *tricked* Cindy into going away suddenly? You know, by faking an emergency call from a sick relative in Seattle or something. Then it wouldn't really be kidnapping, would it?"

"But Cindy would have told someone or left a note that she was going away," Nancy said. "Unless—what if she *did* leave a note, and someone intercepted it? Somebody who lives with her—"

44

"Like Ann Bowers?" Bess completed Nancy's thought. "Do you really think she's responsible, as Cody suggested?"

Nancy looked doubtful. "It could be," she said. "Maybe Cindy *was* giving her trouble—turning down certain campaigns, as Charmaine said—or maybe she knew Cindy was looking for another agent, like Cody seemed to be saying. Then she might have wanted to steer Cindy's work to some of her other models. Didn't Gayle say something about her getting the Healthibits assignment instead of Cindy?"

"That's true," Bess agreed. "And Ms. Bowers did seem kind of edgy when we were talking to her. But she just doesn't seem like a criminal type."

Nancy gave Bess a sideways grin as they turned into the Film Center building. "Bess, you've been on enough cases with me to know that anyone could be 'the criminal type,'" she declared. "But I'll admit, she doesn't seem like the most logical suspect."

Nancy pressed the elevator button to go upstairs. "And then there's the other angle," she went on. "That someone may be sabotaging the Healthibits campaign, not just Cindy. That's what I'd like to look into now."

The girls fell silent, each lost in her own thoughts as they rode the creaking elevator up to the fourth floor.

As they stepped off on four, Nancy caught a

glimpse of something—or someone—moving off to the left. She turned her head, but there was no one in sight.

Had she imagined it, or had someone ducked away when he heard the elevator door opening?

"Excuse me," someone muttered suddenly from her right.

"Oh, sorry." Nancy realized that she was blocking the elevator door. She stepped aside to let a man on. He was tall and skinny, with a receding hairline and weak chin. At first he looked to Nancy like a total nerd, until she noticed the chic style of his baggy olive green suit and black T-shirt.

As the elevator doors closed, he gave Nancy and Bess a careful look, as if trying to place them. Nancy wondered if she'd seen him before. She certainly didn't think so.

Bess rang the buzzer at Studio 4A, and Charmaine came to open the door. Behind her, the door to the soundstage was ajar, but the big room beyond it looked dark and empty. "Carlo decided to send everybody home," Charmaine explained. "There wasn't much else he could do without Cindy."

Nancy heard angry voices from somewhere near the dressing rooms. Glancing at Charmaine, she raised a questioning eyebrow.

"They've been going at it like that for an hour," Charmaine said in an undertone. "It's giving me a headache."

46

Carlo was shouting, "How do I know? Perhaps someone wants me to fail. Perhaps someone wants your cereal to fail. Or perhaps some lunatic hates all people who work in advertising! I am beginning to think that way myself!"

A moment later Carlo came storming out. He noticed Bess and Nancy and stopped, looking ashamed of his outburst. "In my next life I want to be a taxi driver, or a post office clerk," he told them. "But a filmmaker? Never!"

"Did something else happen?" Bess asked.

"Do we need anything else to happen?" Carlo growled. "Cindy has vanished, someone has deliberately tried to wreck the set, and I have three executives shouting in my ears, trying to tell me how to do my job."

Nancy asked, "Carlo, have you given any more thought to who might want to sabotage your work?"

He threw up his hands. "All the world is not my friend, you understand," he declared. "But I didn't think that I had any real enemies." He ran his hands through his bushy gray hair, thinking. "Miklos, now—he does not like me because I fired him. But that was *after* the set fell."

Nancy asked gently, "Who else might want you to fail on this project?"

Carlo glowered darkly. "Well, there is Paul Norman," he confessed. "Another filmmaker. I heard that he was very upset when I was given this assignment. He has done many other cereal commercials, and he knows Cindy—she did two or three screen tests for him. Perhaps he could have convinced her to stay away today."

"Would he be able to get into this studio, to wreck your set?" Nancy asked.

Carlo pursed his lips. "Perhaps," he said. "His offices are in this building, on the ninth floor, and he has used this same studio himself many times. I suppose he could have kept a key."

"What does he look like?" asked Bess.

"Tall, a little bald, with small eyes," Carlo replied. "And no chin."

"Nancy!" Bess said excitedly. "Doesn't that sound like the man we just saw outside in the hallway?"

"I was thinking the same thing," Nancy said. "But if his office is in this building, he no doubt had a good reason to be there. Still, I'd like to ask him some questions. Even if he isn't involved, he might give us a lead. Charmaine, do you have his phone number?"

"Sure thing," Charmaine replied. She flicked on one bank of lights in the soundstage and led Bess and Nancy inside, pushing the door shut behind them. Then she took them over to the telephone and gave Nancy the number of Paul Norman's office.

Nancy dialed, and a man answered. She explained that she wanted to interview Paul Norman for her school paper. The man said that Norman was away from the office but took down

Nancy's name and suggested she try to call again in a couple of hours.

"No luck?" Bess asked as Nancy hung up.

"No, he's out," Nancy reported. "I guess he was on his way out when we saw him."

Just then the telephone rang. Charmaine picked it up and said, "Festa Films, can I help you?"

Nancy noticed her hand suddenly clench the receiver. A moment later Charmaine hung up and turned to Nancy, her face set in an expression of shock.

"Who was it?" Nancy demanded.

"I don't know," Charmaine said slowly. "But whoever it was, he told me to give you two a message."

She licked her lips and repeated the words. "He said that if you and Bess don't go home and mind your own business, you're going to get hurt . . . badly hurt!"

# 6

## A Chase into Darkness

"Nancy, I'm scared," Charmaine continued. She reached out both hands, and Nancy took them. "It didn't sound like an ordinary crank call. And whoever it was, he knew your names, and he knew you were here in the studio."

Nancy rapidly thought about who might know where she and Bess were. Cody, of course, and Ann Bowers. And Paul Norman—*if* that was him they'd seen in the hallway a few minutes ago. He certainly had stared closely at her and Bess as if he knew them.

And there had been someone else in the hallway—Nancy felt sure of it. Who was it?

Bess looked shaken, too. Taking a deep breath, she asked, "Did you recognize the voice? Was it a man or a woman?"

Charmaine blinked a couple of times. "The voice was pretty deep, but I guess it could have been either one." she said. "I'm pretty sure it wasn't anybody I've talked to before, unless he or she was using one of those gadgets to distort your voice."

"Are those very common?" Bess asked.

"Well, my aunt Dahlia, who lives alone, bought herself one last year," Charmaine replied. "She was getting these crank calls that really made her mad. So now when she answers the phone, she sounds like a three-hundred-pound tackle for the Bears. Her friends know it's her and they hang on. But if it's a crank, he usually hangs up after hearing three words."

"What exactly did this caller say?" Nancy asked.

Charmaine frowned. "I don't know if these are the exact words, but it was something like, 'This is a message for those two snoops, Nancy and Bess. They'd better go home and mind their own business before they get badly hurt.'"

"What is this? Who is saying this?"

Nancy looked over her shoulder. Carlo was standing there, his face red with anger.

As soon as Charmaine explained, Carlo exploded. "This is an insult of the worst sort!" he shouted. "Nancy, Bess, you must please ignore all this nonsense. And when I discover who is responsible, I promise he will be very sorry!"

Hearing Carlo's shouting, Stella, Erik, and Sherman Pike came out from the side room

51

where they had been arguing. "What now?" Stella asked as they joined the little group by the phone. "More trouble?"

"Nothing else to hold up the campaign, I hope," Sherman added, rubbing his forehead nervously.

Carlo said, "Charmaine, tell them about the call you just got."

As Charmaine recounted the threatening call, Nancy kept a close eye on her listeners. After all, if someone was sabotaging this ad campaign, any one of these three people might be connected.

Erik looked unimpressed, though Nancy had the feeling that he was listening closely. Stella listened wearily, as if overwhelmed by the recent series of events.

But Sherman Pike's reaction was surprising. "Well?" he demanded, when Charmaine finished. "Why are these two girls here, anyway? What if something happens to them and it gets into the newspapers? The last thing we need is bad publicity. Send them home, right away."

"What will that accomplish?" Carlo asked, with irritation. "Nancy and Bess are experienced detectives, and they know Cindy. I have asked them to find her as quickly as they can. If someone is worried enough to call here with threats, perhaps they are already close to a solution."

Nancy glanced over at Bess. It was nice to hear

Carlo express so much confidence in them. She just wished *she* felt they were that close!

Sherman Pike jutted his chin forward. "But what if they're really working for Amalgamated?" he protested. "They could have arranged that threatening call themselves, to fool us into thinking they're on our side. How do we know who they really are? Cindy's not here to vouch for them, is she?"

"Oh, really, Sherman!" Stella exclaimed. "I think you've been watching too many bad detective shows on TV."

"No, wait a minute," Nancy broke in. She turned to Sherman. "Who is this Amalgamated? And what makes you think they might be responsible for what's been happening?"

The cereal company executive looked nervously right and left, then reached into his pocket for his cigarettes. Catching Charmaine's warning eye on him, he quickly put them back.

"Amalgamated Mills," he muttered. "Our biggest rival. I know for a fact that they've been developing a new cereal product to compete with Healthibits, but we're at least two or three months ahead of them. If we can hold on to that lead, we'll really knock them out of the market. But if they can slow our campaign down, it'll be a whole different ball game."

"And you think that's why they might be trying to delay this commercial?" Bess asked.

53

Sherman shrugged. "It's a theory. That's more than the rest of you seem to have."

"Amalgamated Mills . . ." Carlo said in a far-off voice. "Charmaine, didn't Paul Norman do some work for them last year? Those commercials with old people sailing boats and playing tennis, then eating bowls of cereal?"

"That's Amalgamated, all right," Sherman Pike said quickly. "But who's Paul Norman?"

Erik broke in. "He's a top-notch filmmaker," he said. "I can't believe he'd be involved in anything underhanded. I've worked with him myself, on a couple of accounts. He was always cooperative and professional, and we completed every project on schedule."

As he said this, Erik gave Carlo a sidelong look, as if to add, *Unlike you.* Carlo obviously picked up on the unspoken insult. Nancy saw the color rise in his face and his fists clench by his sides.

But before Carlo could speak, Stella stepped between him and Erik. "This constant bickering has just got to stop," she said firmly. "We all have to pull together on this project. Do you hear me? Otherwise, I'm afraid I'll have to ask you to leave, Erik."

Erik seemed to realize that he had gone too far. "Don't get me wrong, Stella," he said. "I want McVie and Martin to keep this account, just as much as you do. In fact—"

Nancy stopped listening to Erik's semi-apology.

The other side of the soundstage was still in shadows, but suddenly, near the entrance, she noticed a wedge of light spilling across the floor from the entry hall.

Hadn't that door been closed before? she thought intently. And what was that bumpy shadow along one edge of the triangle of light?

Was someone standing just outside that doorway, eavesdropping?

Nancy nudged Bess with her elbow, then tipped her head to draw Bess's attention to the doorway. Bess looked, then met Nancy's eyes and nodded silently.

The two slipped away from the little knot of arguers and walked quietly toward the door. They were about twenty feet away when the pool of light suddenly narrowed, then disappeared.

Someone had just closed the door.

"Come on," Nancy murmured, dashing forward. She tugged the door open and ran into the entry hall and then out into the corridor. There was no one in sight.

Then Nancy looked at the elevator. Above the door, the arrow pointing to the floor numbers was moving downward from four.

Recalling how slowly the elevator moved, Nancy said, "Quick, Bess—the stairs. We'll head him off downstairs!"

Pushing through a nearby door, the girls found a set of wide marble stairs. As they clattered down them, Nancy caught a glimpse of a stained-glass skylight far above. She made a mental note to come back for a closer look sometime—when she wasn't busy chasing a suspicious character.

Reaching the bottom of the stairs, Nancy burst through sculpted bronze doors into the lobby. She dashed over to the elevator. It was still on its way down. "We've got him," she said as Bess caught up to her, panting. "In a few seconds, we'll know who was trying to listen."

They glued their eyes on the brass arrow. It reached L. Then, instead of stopping, it continued to move toward B.

"The basement?" Bess gasped. "But those stairs we came down don't go any farther!"

"There must be another set," Nancy said, turning to scan the lobby. On the wall opposite the elevator was a framed diagram of the floor. She hurried over and studied it swiftly, then led Bess to another bronze door in the far corner. As usual the doorman took no notice.

Behind the door was a narrower set of stairs, made of concrete instead of marble. Nancy and Bess ran down them. At the bottom, a steel fire door blocked the way. Nancy took a deep breath and pushed. The door creaked open.

She stepped through cautiously, with Bess close behind her. They found themselves inside a large, dimly lit open area. Several doors led off from the room, and a row of large trash bins on wheels rested next to what was apparently a service elevator. Otherwise the basement was completely empty. They could see into every corner, and no one was there.

The passenger elevator stood beside them, its doors wide open. Nancy hurried over to look inside. It was empty, too.

"We know he came down to the basement," Bess said. "The elevator didn't stop once on the way down here. Whoever was in it *must* be down here somewhere!"

"If there *was* someone in it," Nancy replied. "We didn't actually see him, did we? What if the eavesdropper pushed the button inside the elevator, then slipped out and hid around a corner while we chased down the stairs?"

"He'd have to be an awfully fast sprinter to do that," Bess said doubtfully.

"I agree," Nancy said. "Let's not give up the chase yet. Where do all these doors go, do you think?"

As Nancy and Bess circled the room, they saw that most of the doors were padlocked shut. Thick dust lay on the doorknobs, proving that no one had touched them in a long time. One opened, but it led into a small, dusty storage closet.

They had nearly completed the round when Bess whispered, "Nancy, look—that door has no padlock. And the doorknob's clean!"

Nancy bent down to look. A few rough swipes had rubbed away much of the dust, in a pattern that looked like gripping fingers.

She pushed the door. After a moment's resistance, it swung inward with a groan of rusty hinges.

"Bess, look," Nancy said excitedly, "a hidden staircase! Where do you suppose it leads?"

"To someplace dark and dank and full of cobwebs," Bess said, shuddering. "Do we really have to go down there, Nancy?"

"You can stay here and keep watch while I check it out," Nancy suggested.

Bess groaned, then said, "No, I'm coming. But don't ask me to pretend I like it."

Nancy led the way down into the dim, chilly stairwell. A damp earth smell grew stronger at every step. At the bottom of the stairs was a rusty metal door. Nancy pushed it open.

The space on the other side was almost totally dark. The light from the open doorway showed a filthy concrete floor and two brick walls that arched inward to form a vaulted ceiling. Ahead of them, the darkness seemed to stretch out forever.

"Nancy, where are we?" Bess whispered fearfully. "This place is totally weird."

"The abandoned freight tunnels!" Nancy whispered back. "I saw a story about them on TV last year. They run under most of downtown Chicago. Coal used to be delivered through them to heat the buildings. Now they're only used for telephone lines and stuff like that."

"Nancy?" Bess said softly. "I just saw something move—down there." She pointed, with a shaking finger.

Nancy looked. Far ahead of them, a faint glow of light bobbed up and down in the darkness. Someone walking with a flashlight, Nancy guessed. Straining her ears, she could make out a soft sound like footsteps.

"Let's get him," she breathed to Bess.

They set off into the pitch darkness, using a heel-and-toe step that combined swiftness and silence. Nancy was in the lead.

But she hadn't gone more than twenty feet when suddenly Bess gave a bloodcurdling scream!

# 7

## A Clue in the Dust

As soon as Bess screamed, the light they had been pursuing went out.

"Bess, are you all right?" Nancy called into the darkness.

Bess whimpered softly. "I stepped on something and—it moved," she said in a plaintive voice. "I'm sure it was a rat!"

As if to confirm her fears, tiny scrabbling noises rose from the dirt and debris on the tunnel floor. Bess gasped and grabbed Nancy's arm.

Then, farther down the tunnel, a clanging boom echoed off the brick walls. It sounded like a heavy door slamming shut.

Nancy's shoulders sagged in disappointment. She realized that she couldn't blame Bess for screaming, but it was frustrating to know that their suspect had escaped.

"Nancy, I'm sorry," Bess said miserably. "I couldn't help it. I hate rats."

"It's okay," Nancy replied, slipping her arm around Bess's quivering shoulders. "Without a flashlight, I doubt if we could have caught our eavesdropper anyway. Come on—let's see if we can find our way back to the daylight world."

A faint rectangle of light outlined the door they had come through. They slipped back through it into the murky stairway. Nancy started up, then stopped so suddenly that Bess bumped into her from behind.

"What is it?" Bess demanded, grabbing Nancy tensely. "Another rat?"

"No," Nancy replied, backing away from the stairs. "But I do see a pretty clear footprint in the dust, and I'm sure neither of us made it."

Digging into her jeans pocket, Nancy found a ballpoint pen and the slip of paper Charmaine had given her with Ann Bowers's address on it. On the back, she started to make a rough sketch of the footprint. "The person we were after is wearing running shoes," she reported. "It's a brand I've never heard of—Ourson."

"If you've never heard of it, how do you know the name?" Bess asked, puzzled.

Nancy grinned and pointed to the footprint. "Elementary, my dear Bess. The name is molded into the sole of the shoe," she explained.

She bent down and used the edge of the paper to measure the print. "Somewhere around a size ten," she added. "I wonder if many stores in Chicago carry Ourson shoes."

"Let's go ask Charmaine," Bess suggested. "She's really up on fashion."

"We should also find out if many people know about this entrance to the tunnels," Nancy said. "Whoever we were chasing sure didn't come down here by accident. He or she knew exactly where to go."

Nancy and Bess continued up the stairs to the basement level and rang for the elevator. As they rode back up to the fourth floor, Bess thought out loud, "Why would he—or she—go to the trouble of leaving by the freight tunnel? Why not simply walk out the front entrance?"

"Because he wanted to be sure nobody saw him here," Nancy suggested. "And come to think of it, I guess we don't need to say 'he or she'—very few women wear a shoe that big."

"That means Ann Bowers wasn't our eavesdropper," Bess concluded. "No surprise. Somehow, I couldn't see her prowling around downstairs in all that dirt anyway. She might break a nail or something."

Upstairs, Charmaine met them at the door to the studio. Before they could ask her about the shoe brand, she silenced them with a warning look. "Brace yourselves," she muttered out of the side of her mouth. "Trouble ahead."

Carlo saw them and came over. Looking shamefaced, he said, "I have been told to ask you to leave. I am sorry, but . . ."

"Asked by whom?" Nancy replied calmly.

"Mr. Pike says there is no mystery here for you to solve," Carlo told her, with a slight shrug. "He feels that Cindy has simply broken her contract. And he worries that your investigation will only create bad publicity for his product."

"That's ridiculous!" Bess said loudly. "What about that set wall falling over? What does that have to do with Cindy's contract?"

Nancy nudged Bess with her elbow. She could tell from Carlo's manner that he had been pressured into this decision. "We understand," she said. "We have to get back to River Heights anyway. But I'll give you my phone number, just in case you want to get in touch with me."

Carlo, looking relieved, tucked the number in his pocket and turned away.

"Nancy, how can we quit, just like that?" Bess muttered fiercely after the director walked away. "We can't just abandon Cindy."

"Later," Nancy murmured, heading for the door.

Once they were on the street, Nancy picked up the conversation. "Look, Bess, we can't force Carlo to let us hang around," she pointed out. "Besides, this may be a good thing for the investigation."

"How could it be good?" Bess asked skeptically.

"If everyone thinks we've given up, maybe the

63

culprit will get overconfident and make a blunder," Nancy said. "And meanwhile, we have plenty of detective work to do."

That night at home, before going to bed, Nancy called Ann Bowers to ask if there was any news of Cindy. "I'm afraid not," Ms. Bowers replied with a sigh. "I called the police and the hospitals again an hour ago, but they had nothing to report. I must say, the police didn't seem terribly concerned."

"A lot of people occasionally drop out of sight for a day or two," Nancy told her. "The police generally don't start really looking until someone's been gone for forty-eight hours."

"Well, that won't bring Cindy back in time to make this commercial," Ms. Bowers complained. "I'll have to have a serious talk with Stella first thing tomorrow, to try to save the situation." After promising to let Nancy know the moment there were any new developments, Ms. Bowers hung up.

Bess arrived at the Drew house before eight o'clock the next morning, carrying a box of fresh doughnuts. Nancy's father, attorney Carson Drew, was leaving for the office, but he paused long enough to sample a doughnut.

"Excellent," he said, a twinkle in his eye. "I'm sure you two are planning to leave some for later—when I get home, for example."

64

Nancy was making a pot of tea. "We'll make a point of it, Dad," she promised with a laugh.

She and Bess sat at the breakfast table. "What next?" Bess asked, between bites of a jelly doughnut.

"We need to talk to Cindy's mom," Nancy replied. "I called her last night and set up a time to meet her. She's pretty upset and worried, but she agreed to talk to us. As she told Ms. Bowers yesterday, she hasn't heard from Cindy. But maybe she can tell us more about Cindy's state of mind—whether she'd be likely to run away from this job, for instance."

"Do you really think that's possible?" Bess asked. "There sure are lots of people who have a motive to keep Cindy from doing the commercials. Cody wanted her to drop the campaign, even if he says he wouldn't have stood in her way. Ann Bowers may have thought Cindy was going to leave her for another agent. And what about someone who's using Cindy to hurt Carlo—that guy Miklos, for example? Or someone from Amalgamated Cereals, trying to sink the whole project?"

"Amalgamated Mills," Nancy corrected her friend. "And that's not such a far-out idea. What if Miklos was being paid by Amalgamated? He could easily have sabotaged the set. He could even have lured Cindy someplace by calling with a change of plans—she wouldn't doubt one of Carlo's assistants. And he might have been our eavesdropper yesterday. Working in the building, he would probably know about that tunnel."

"Nancy, that's brilliant. It all fits!" Bess exclaimed, waving her second doughnut excitedly.

Nancy smiled and brushed specks of powdered sugar off her sleeve. "Yes, but at this point we could come up with three or four other scenarios that fit just as well," she said. "We need more facts before we can really narrow down the possibilities."

After finishing breakfast, the girls got into Nancy's blue Mustang and headed for the Sunderland house. Mrs. Sunderland lived in a small split-level house in one of the older subdivisions of River Heights. Nancy parked in the driveway, and she and Bess followed the neat stone walk up to the front steps.

Mrs. Sunderland opened the door even before they had a chance to ring the doorbell. She was in her early forties, with shoulder-length brown hair and arresting blue eyes. Cindy had clearly inherited her good looks from her mother. But Mrs. Sunderland's face looked creased with worry, and her eyes were rimmed with red as if she had been crying.

"Please come in," she said. "I'm so glad you came. You two girls are my best hope for finding Cindy."

"You haven't heard anything further?" Nancy asked as they followed her into the living room.

"Nothing," Cindy's mother replied, wringing her hands and sinking down into an armchair. "I'm worried sick. I wanted to go up to Chicago myself, but Ann Bowers said I should stay here, in case Cindy came or called me here."

Nancy and Bess exchanged a glance. Did Ann Bowers have some other reason for keeping Cindy's mother out of the way?

"It's so distressing," Mrs. Sunderland went on. "Just when Cindy's career was going so well . . ."

"How did she feel about her big break?" Bess asked. "Her friend Gayle said she seemed awfully nervous."

"Nervous? Of course, who wouldn't be?" Mrs. Sunderland replied. "But she was also thrilled. She couldn't wait to get started. When she came down with a head cold a couple of weeks ago, she acted as though it was the end of the world. You see, she was afraid it might cause problems with the campaign." A brave smile lit up Mrs. Sunderland's face. "If you can't taste anything, it's a lot harder to look excited about eating cereal, I guess."

"May we look at Cindy's room?" Nancy asked.

Mrs. Sunderland stood up. "Sure, if you think it'll help," she said. "It's this way."

The room, at the end of a short hall, looked like something from a catalog. The bedspread, curtains, and wallpaper were all in the same pattern of yellow roses. Stuffed animals were lined up on

67

a long shelf under the windows. On the dresser stood an array of tiny sampler bottles of designer perfumes.

In the distance, the telephone rang, and Mrs. Sunderland jumped. "Uh, make yourselves at home," she said anxiously. "I'll be right back."

Bess began looking through the dresser drawers. Nancy peered into the closet, which was mostly empty, then wandered into the adjoining bathroom. Like Cindy's bathroom in Chicago, it held an astonishing collection of shampoos and body lotions, as well as herbal cold remedies, vitamins, and allergy medicines.

"Nancy!" Mrs. Sunderland suddenly called from the bedroom doorway. Her face was pale, and she gripped the edge of the door tensely. "Would you get on the phone, please? It's . . . it's Ann Bowers. I'm afraid she's had bad news."

Nancy hurried out into the hall and picked up the receiver. "This is Nancy. What is it?"

"Nancy, can you and Bess come back to Chicago right away?" Ms. Bowers said, in a voice that trembled. "I need your help. Someone just called me. He said that he's one of the people who've kidnapped Cindy."

Holding the phone tightly, Nancy asked, "Did you actually speak to Cindy?"

"No," Ms. Bowers replied. "But just before he hung up, I—I heard someone scream. I'm sure it was Cindy!"

# 8

# Kidnapped!

Nancy was silent for a moment, as she tried to take in Ms. Bowers's news about Cindy.

Ms. Bowers filled the silence. "There's a guest room in the apartment that you and Bess can stay in," she offered. "Please, tell me you'll come as soon as possible."

"I'll talk it over with Bess and let you know," Nancy said. "Here's Cindy's mom again."

Nancy handed the receiver to Mrs. Sunderland, then took Bess aside and filled her in. Meanwhile, Mrs. Sunderland kept nodding numbly as she talked to Ann Bowers. Finally she said goodbye and dropped the receiver back onto the cradle. She looked stunned. Bess helped her to a seat.

"I don't understand," Mrs. Sunderland moaned. "Why would someone kidnap my baby? She never did anything to hurt anybody. And why did they call Ann Bowers? Why not me?"

Nancy had been wondering that, too. "Which address is on Cindy's ID?" she asked. "This one, or the one in Chicago?"

"I have no idea," Cindy's mom admitted. "Chicago, I suppose. You think maybe the kidnappers didn't know where to reach me?"

"It's possible," Nancy told her. "There are a lot of questions about this. But I promise we're going to do our best to find the answers—and to find Cindy."

Mrs. Sunderland leaned forward to grasp Nancy's hand. "Is there anything I could do to help?"

Nancy gave her hand a comforting squeeze. "I think Ms. Bowers is right. You should stay here, in case someone tries to contact you," she said. "If there's any reason for you to come to Chicago, we'll call you at once."

"And what about notifying the police? The FBI?" Cindy's mom continued, sounding more and more distraught.

"I think that's something you ought to talk over with Ms. Bowers," Nancy said gently. "She knows the situation better than we do at this point."

Nancy used Mrs. Sunderland's phone to call her dad, then Bess called her mother. Both quickly gave permission for the two teens to return immediately to Chicago.

"But keep in touch with me—and be careful,"

Carson Drew warned, before saying goodbye. "Kidnappers are dangerous criminals."

Nancy called Ms. Bowers back with the news, then told Mrs. Sunderland, "We're on our way now. Wish us luck."

"I do, I do," Cindy's mother replied. "Just get my little girl back!"

It was after eleven when Nancy parked her blue Mustang on a side street near Ann Bowers's building. She and Bess grabbed their overnight bags from the backseat and walked inside. The doorman recognized them and smiled. "Oh, yes. Ms. Bowers called down to say that you'll be staying a few days," he said.

Upstairs, Nancy rang the bell. To her surprise, Cody Charles answered the door. His expression was somber.

"Thanks for agreeing to help," he said.

"Ms. Bowers told you about the phone call?" Bess asked.

"Yep," he said. "But it was no surprise. I'd already got a call myself. I almost managed to tape it, but it took me too long to remember which button to punch on my answering machine."

Bess and Nancy followed him into the living room, where Ms. Bowers jumped up to greet them. "I can't tell you how relieved I am to see you girls," she said. "I have no idea what to do.

71

Thank goodness Gayle was here when I got that terrible call. Otherwise, I'm sure I would have collapsed on the spot."

"What do the police say?" Nancy asked.

"Well . . ." Ms. Bowers said, her voice trailing off.

Cody jumped in. "I feel strongly that we shouldn't bring in the authorities yet," he said. "The person who called me said that if I told the police, it would be bad for Cindy."

"Kidnappers usually say that," Nancy pointed out. "But the authorities will know how to deal with them. They've had a lot more experience than you or me."

"Oh, I know," Cody replied, seeming troubled. "But I just don't think we should make a move too soon."

"Cody pointed out something else," Ms. Bowers added. "Once the police are involved, there'll be no way to hush up this incident. And I'm afraid it could have a serious effect on Cindy's career."

"Being kidnapped is bad publicity?" Bess asked in a skeptical tone.

"I'm not sure it fits in with the wholesome image the Healthibits girl should have," Ms. Bowers replied solemnly. "Though of course it's not her fault, this kind of thing could hurt her image in the business as a reliable girl. I discussed this with Cindy's mother, and she agrees with me."

"I don't like it," Nancy said slowly. "But I'll go along, for the time being."

"Thanks," Cody said, with an audible sigh of relief. "Listen, I have to go, but you have my number, right? Please, call me the instant you learn anything."

After he left, Ms. Bowers sighed. "At least there's one good thing about getting that terrible phone call," she said. "It gives me some ammunition in case McVie and Martin tries to invoke the escape clause and fire Cindy. They wouldn't dare penalize a kidnapping victim that way."

Nancy caught Bess's eye. She could see they both had the same thought. Whether she realized it or not, Ms. Bowers had just admitted that she had a strong motive to invent the kidnappers' call—it was a perfect way to protect her client's career. Had Gayle really been there when Ms. Bowers got the call? Nancy made a mental note to question the young model later.

"What did the kidnappers say about ransom?" Nancy asked Ms. Bowers.

Ann Bowers looked surprised, as if the question hadn't occurred to her. "Why, nothing at all," she replied.

Nancy gave Bess another glance. No ransom demand? Then why had Cindy been kidnapped?

"Perhaps they're waiting for our anxiety level to rise before they discuss money," Ms. Bowers mused. "And they must know I'm not her parent—maybe they wanted to give me a chance to contact her mother."

"When it comes down to that," Nancy put in, "why *didn't* they contact Mrs. Sunderland? Surely they could force Cindy to give them her home number." Nancy winced inwardly. It was scary to think of Cindy being pressed for information at the hands of her kidnappers.

Ms. Bowers fidgeted. "It is mysterious, isn't it?" she said—then gave a shrug. "Well, that's why you're here. Let me show you your room. Oh, remind me to give you a set of apartment keys. And you'll need a magnetic card that lets you into the garage, so you can park your car down there."

As she led them down the hallway, Nancy wondered why Ms. Bowers seemed so eager to change the subject. A lot of things about this supposed kidnapping just didn't add up.

After she and Bess had dropped their bags in the guest room, Nancy said, "Ms. Bowers, I'd like another look at Cindy's room. Can you come with us? You might notice something that we'd otherwise miss."

"Of course, dear," Ms. Bowers replied.

Cindy's room looked just as it had the day before. "Bess, this time you take the bathroom and I'll search this room," Nancy suggested.

"Okay," Bess replied.

Nancy went to work on the dresser, opening each drawer in turn and sifting carefully through

74

the neatly piled clothing. When she was finished, all she had learned was that Cindy had a lot of nice clothes. She was about to start looking through the wastebasket when Ms. Bowers said from the doorway, "I wonder where Wilbur is?"

"Who's Wilbur?" Nancy asked, puzzled.

"Cindy's favorite stuffed animal," Ms. Bowers replied. "A very cute pink pig. He's Cindy's good-luck charm. I don't see him anywhere."

Nancy scanned the shelf of animals, then kneeled down to peer under the bed. No pink pig.

"Was Cindy in the habit of taking Wilbur with her wherever she went?" Nancy asked, intrigued.

"As a mascot, you mean?" said Ms. Bowers. "Not as a rule, no. But yesterday was a special day. She would have taken him with her for luck."

Nancy nodded. "If he's not here, maybe that proves she was headed for the studio when she left the apartment," she mused.

"Nancy, I've found something," Bess called from the bathroom. She came out, holding a narrow piece of flimsy paper.

"Look," she said. "This is a receipt from an herbalist's shop. Last week Cindy spent nearly two hundred dollars there."

"Really? On what?" Nancy asked.

"I don't know, I can't read the writing," Bess said. "But doesn't that sound like an awful lot to spend on herbs?"

Ms. Bowers smiled. "Cindy goes in for different health fads," she explained. "A lot of the girls do—I guess because they're so body-conscious. Gayle always teases Cindy about it."

"That's an awful lot to spend on a fad," Nancy said. "Maybe she was looking for something healthy to calm her nerves before the commercial shoot. Anyway, I think we'd better check this out."

She put the receipt in her pocket, then picked up a small photo of Cindy from the dresser top. "Can I take this?" she asked Ms. Bowers. "It might help us when we're questioning people."

Ms. Bowers nodded. "Anything you want."

After saying goodbye to the modeling agent, Nancy and Bess went down to where they had parked the Mustang. Checking a map of the city, Nancy found the location of the herbal shop. They set off, driving south to Chicago Avenue, then turning west.

"This neighborhood has certainly been around awhile," Bess said. "Look at all the old brick buildings."

"Yes," Nancy said. "And look at all the new restaurants and trendy boutiques in them. I guess old is hip. Hey, we're in luck—there's a parking space."

She backed into the space, and she and Bess got out. Delicious smells from a nearby pizza shop tempted them to stop briefly for a lunch of Chicago-style deep-dish pizza. Then, on foot, they proceeded a block to the street they were looking for.

Barely wider than an alley, it sloped down toward the river. The brick building on the corner was being renovated, leaving dirt and mud all over the pavement. They walked under the scaffolding, dodging around a couple of Dumpsters loaded with construction debris, and started down the street.

"That's the place," Bess said, pointing to a small shop across the street. Hand-printed signs in the front window advertised Nature's Herbal Cures for weight, complexion, allergy, and memory problems.

As they entered the shop, the mixture of smells made Nancy feel as if she were drowning in a cup of herb tea. The man behind the counter was tall and thin, with a long brown ponytail and striking blue eyes. He wore jeans and a bright tie-dyed T-shirt. "What can I do for you?" he asked in a mellow voice.

"Our friend, Cindy, bought a lot of stuff here the other day," said Nancy. She pulled the receipt from her pocket. As if by chance, she let Cindy's photo fall on the counter. She didn't want to make it obvious that she was investigating a crime.

"Hey, that's her picture," she said, picking it up and showing it to the man. "Do you remember her?"

"Oh, for sure," he answered. "She's a steady

customer. Besides, I've seen her picture all over, on posters and stuff. Sometimes when she comes in, I kid her about how she ought to do ads for some of our antiallergy products."

"Is that what she bought?" Nancy asked.

The man took the receipt and glanced at it. "Yes, this is all for allergies, hay fever, cold symptoms, like that," he said. "Oh, and she tried our special genko extract. They say it helps promote better brain-stem functioning. You want to give that a try?"

Nancy laughed. "I'm not a hundred percent sure what my brain stem does, but I think it's doing it okay," she said. "You know, this seems like a lot of money for Cindy to spend just to cure that cold of hers."

"*And* her allergies," the man pointed out.

"Well, I'm not allergic to anything," Nancy said. "I was hoping to buy whatever she uses to counteract stress. She always looks so calm and radiant, you know?"

The man nodded. "That's inner peace," he said. "We haven't learned how to bottle that yet."

"Well, thanks, anyway," Nancy said brightly.

Outside, as they started back across the narrow street, Bess complained, "That was a waste of time."

"Not totally," Nancy said. "He said that none of that stuff Cindy bought was for her nerves. But if she was really as stressed out as Gayle says she was—"

Nancy stopped in midsentence. What was that squealing noise? She looked over her shoulder.

Her eyes widened, and she caught her breath. One of the big wheeled Dumpsters was bumping down the narrow street in their direction.

Turning, Bess saw it too and gasped. It was hurtling straight at them!

# 9

## A Narrow Escape

As the heavy Dumpster rumbled down the street, Nancy shouted, "Quick, Bess! Out of the way!"

Bess screamed and flung herself to one side. Nancy leapt to the other side. But her foot slipped into a pothole, wrenching her ankle. She felt herself lurch forward—right into the path of the Dumpster! She flung her hands over her head to protect herself as she fell helplessly to the ground.

Just then the Dumpster hit a hump in the pavement. It careened wildly across the narrow street and crashed into the side of a parked car.

"Oh, no!" The herbalist came running out of his shop. "My car! What a bummer!"

Then he noticed Nancy and Bess sprawled on the sidewalk. "Are you guys okay?" he asked.

"I'm okay," Bess mumbled. She still looked a little dazed.

Nancy stood up, testing her ankle. "I'm fine,"

she said. "At least that thing didn't flatten me."
Reassured, the herbalist went over to check out
the damage on his car.

Nancy looked at Bess. "I wonder how that
Dumpster happened to roll down the street just
as we came out of the shop," she said.

"It *is* a pretty strange coincidence," Bess
agreed.

They crossed the street to look at the big metal
container. Nancy knelt down and studied the
wide steel wheels. "See that?" she said to Bess.
"The wheels at one end have simple brakes built
into them. Either they weren't set properly . . ."

"Or somebody deliberately released them,"
Bess said, finishing Nancy's sentence. "Then
whoever it was gave the thing a shove to start it
down the street in our direction. Thank goodness
we had plenty of time to get out of the way."

Nancy nodded. "Whoever did it was more
interested in sending us a warning than in really
hurting us," she speculated. "Though he or she
obviously didn't care if we *did* get hurt."

"Look what that thing did to my car!" the guy
from the store exclaimed. "Do you have any idea
who did this?"

"Sorry, no," Nancy told him. "But if we find
out, we'll let you know. Come on, Bess. Let's go
look at where the Dumpster was parked before it
went on its joyride."

As she and Bess walked up the block toward
the corner, Nancy studied the street. The

Dumpster had left faint muddy tracks on the pavement. As they approached the spot where the other Dumpster was still parked, Nancy caught her breath.

The mud in the gutter was trampled, as if someone had stepped all over it. And just next to the curb was a clear footprint.

Nancy went down on one knee and studied it. Then she rummaged through her shoulder bag. She pulled out the sketch she had made the day before, on the stairs down to the freight tunnel.

Bess, peering over her shoulder, said, "Nancy! They're the same shoe!"

Nancy nodded grimly. "It looks that way," she said. "Whoever rolled that Dumpster at us is probably our eavesdropper from yesterday."

"But how did he know we were here?" Bess wondered.

"Ann Bowers and Cody Charles were the only people who knew that we were back in town," Nancy pointed out. "At least I think they were."

Bess looked dubious. "I can't imagine Ann Bowers wearing sneakers," she said. "She's more the type for expensive Italian slingbacks. Besides, as you said yesterday, this shoe is too big for most women."

"She could have hired someone else to do it," Nancy said. "What if she invented this whole kidnapping plot to cover up for Cindy's running away? Giving us a scare would make it all even more believable."

"But Cody got a call from the kidnapper, too," Bess objected.

"That could have been Ann, using one of those voice distorters," said Nancy. "Look, there's a pay phone on the corner. Let's call to see if she's home."

A couple of minutes later, she hung up and turned to Bess. "Well," she said, "I talked to Gayle. She said Ms. Bowers was on the other line, talking to some designer in Milan. And according to Gayle, she's been home, on the phone, for at least the last half hour. I wonder if she was lining up somebody to attack us?"

Bess looked worried. Nancy knew what she was thinking: they were staying in this woman's apartment. If she was determined to hurt them, she'd have plenty of opportunities.

Nancy went on. "I tried to question Gayle, but she was on her way out. She said she's working on a commercial this afternoon—at the Film Center, Studio 6B. I persuaded her to talk to us there."

Nancy and Bess got back in the Mustang and drove to the Film Center. They found their way up to Studio 6B and rang the bell.

A young woman in a black leather miniskirt opened the door. "Come on in," she said softly, "but don't make any noise."

She led them inside. The studio was a bit smaller and more cluttered than the one Carlo was using. The set was decorated to look like a suburban living room. Half a dozen teenage girls in pajamas were sprawled on the floor around a huge bowl of popcorn.

One of them was Gayle. She looked up, noticed Bess and Nancy, and waved. Then another girl playfully threw a fluffy kernel of popcorn at her. Gayle giggled and threw one back.

Bess tugged urgently on Nancy's sleeve. Nancy looked to where she was pointing and halted in surprise.

A tall, thin man was bending down to peer through the viewfinder of the camera. When he straightened up and looked around, Nancy recognized him.

It was the same man she and Bess had noticed in the hall outside Carlo's studio the day before.

"Paul, come check this out," a lighting director called to him. Nancy and Bess exchanged glances. So it *was* Carlo's rival, Paul Norman!

Nancy swiftly glanced at his shoes. She felt a touch of disappointment. He was wearing brown tassel loafers without socks, not Ourson running shoes.

Gayle's boyfriend, Jason, was standing on the other side of the set. He noticed Nancy and Bess and came around to join them.

"Gayle asked me to come, for moral support," he whispered. "She's really upset about Cindy's being kidnapped. Upset, and scared, too."

Before Nancy or Bess could reply, Paul Norman called out, "Okay, everybody, five-minute break. But, girls, stay on the set. I don't want you to lose that pose now." Looking over his shoulder, he added, "Porfirio? Start another big batch of popcorn, please. The aroma helps to create just the right mood."

He beckoned to the young woman who had answered the door. He spoke to her briefly, then looked over at Nancy and Bess, his eyes narrowing. He walked over to them. "You must be the girls Gayle had asked to meet her here," he said. "You're detectives?"

"Yes. We need to talk to Gayle for a couple of minutes," Nancy replied. "But could we ask you a few questions first about Cindy Sunderland?"

Norman raised his eyebrows. "Cindy? Why not ask Carlo Festa? He's using her in the new campaign he's filming, you know." His voice had a sarcastic ring.

"We know," Bess said. "But Cindy didn't turn up for the first day of filming. No one knows where she is or what's happened to her."

"Well, *I* certainly don't," Paul Norman told her. He looked surprisingly unconcerned. "I don't think I've seen her for weeks and weeks."

Nancy took a deep breath. "Was it a big disappointment when Carlo was given those cereal commercials instead of you?" she asked.

Norman stiffened. "Who told you—" he began, then broke off with an exaggerated shrug. "Half the people in this business live only to gossip," he scoffed. "No, it wasn't a big disappointment. A very tiny one, frankly. Carlo lucked out this time, but luck goes around. It was not a big deal at all."

Bess started to ask another question, but Norman held up a hand like a traffic cop. "Sorry, girls, I have to get back to work," he said. "The future of American popcorn is riding on my talent."

He turned and strode back to the set, cupping his hands around his mouth to call, "Places, please! Places, everyone!"

"We won't be able to talk to Gayle until she's finished shooting," Nancy murmured. "Let's go down to see Carlo. He probably gave everyone the day off, since Cindy's still not back. If Sherman Pike's not there, we can discuss the case with him."

As they walked down two flights, Nancy recalled chasing the eavesdropper down into the freight tunnels the day before. Did many people know about the tunnel access in the basement of the building? she wondered again.

Coming out on the fourth floor, Nancy and Bess headed for the door to Studio 4A. Suddenly it opened and Miklos stepped out.

The girls halted in surprise. Miklos glowered at them and brushed past.

"Mr. Personality," Bess murmured when the door to the stairway closed behind him. "What's he doing here? I thought Carlo fired him."

"Maybe Carlo took him back," Nancy suggested. She rapped on the studio door, which was still ajar, and then pushed it open. They passed into the soundstage.

To their surprise, the room was full of people and activity. The crew was milling busily around the set. Nancy noticed Stella, Erik, and Sherman Pike across the room. They seemed too involved in their discussion to notice the girls. Maybe it was better that way, she thought.

"Oh, hi, guys," Charmaine said, joining them. "Wow, what a coincidence! Carlo was just saying that he had to call you. He felt really bad about chasing you away yesterday. He's managed to convince Mr. Pike that you could be helpful after all."

"That's nice," Nancy replied. "Say, wasn't that Miklos we just saw leaving?"

Charmaine nodded. "Yeah, he came by to pick up some stuff he'd left here." She seemed about to say more, but at that moment Carlo hurried over.

"You are back," he said happily. "Is there news of Cindy?"

"I'm afraid not," Nancy told him.

Carlo's face fell. Shaking his head, he turned to his assistant. "Charmaine, make sure that everyone is ready," he said. Charmaine nodded, threw Nancy and Bess a parting smile, and walked away.

"We are shooting parts of the commercial in which Cindy does not appear," the director

87

explained. "This way, we do not lose so much time." He glanced around and lowered his voice. "I called Ann Bowers just now. She says Cindy has been kidnapped. Is it true?"

"It looks that way," Nancy said, careful not to reveal her own doubts.

"I wish I knew what to do," Carlo said. "This commercial is on a very strict schedule. Unless Cindy is found quickly, I am afraid that the ad agency will decide to replace her."

"Do you have other good candidates for the job?" asked Bess.

"Oh, yes, two or three, though no one who is as right for the part as Cindy is," Carlo replied. "Her friend Gayle, for example, is not bad."

Charmaine hurried over. "Everyone's ready, Carlo," she announced.

"Ah. Thank you." To Bess and Nancy, he said, "Excuse me. You may watch if it interests you."

He walked over to the set. There was a blaze of light as the big floodlights were turned on.

Nancy sniffed the air and frowned. "Do you smell something funny?" she asked Bess.

Before her friend could answer, Nancy saw a billow of gray smoke pour out from behind the set. The shrill clamor of a smoke alarm pierced the air.

"Fire!" someone shouted. *"Fire!"*

# 10

# Fire!

Acrid fumes spread rapidly through the studio. Coughing and gasping, people started to rush toward the door.

Nancy held up her arms and shouted, "Calm down, everybody! Walk! Don't run!"

A man in a black leather vest stared at her blankly as he pushed past. Nancy remembered him—Stefan, the food stylist. He looked as if he was on the edge of panic.

"Come on, Nancy," Bess urged, yanking at her arm. "Let's get out of here."

Grabbing their coats and purses, Nancy and Bess headed for the exit, looking around as they went. Carlo and one of the technical crew ran past in the opposite direction, toward the source of the smoke. Carlo was carrying a small, bright red fire extinguisher.

Outside, in the hallway, Charmaine was helping direct people toward the stairs. "Take it easy, folks," she kept repeating loudly. "There's no danger. Just take it easy."

A stream of people from the higher floors filled the stairs. Nancy and Bess waited for a gap, then joined them. They were nearly at the lobby level when the crowd started squeezing against the wall. Three firefighters in rubber coats and breathing masks came rushing up the stairs. Behind them were two police officers, who began guiding people out onto the sidewalk.

Bess and Nancy followed the crowd to stand behind some temporary police barricades. A couple of minutes later, Nancy saw Carlo come out of the building, looking tired and upset. He saw the girls and came over to join them.

"Absolutely nothing goes right with this job," he moaned.

"Is there much damage upstairs?" Bess asked anxiously.

"Pah! It is nothing," Carlo replied. "Some fool left a plastic shopping bag on top of one of the lighting transformers. When we turned on the lights, the transformer heated up and the bag melted. That's what made that terrible smoke.

"At least the idiot has good taste," he added with a rueful smile. "The bag was from Sargent's, in Lake Forest. A very chic store."

"I'm surprised that there isn't a sprinkler system in the studio," Nancy said.

"There is," Carlo told her. "But it is set off by high temperatures, not by smoke. When plastic burns, it gives off a thick black smoke, which simply clogs the sprinkler heads. Actually, that is one bit of luck for me. If the sprinklers had gone off, they would have destroyed the set and all our equipment."

The firefighters began filing out again. Carlo went over and spoke to one who seemed to be in charge. He came back shaking his head gloomily.

"They say we must wait at least half an hour for the air-conditioning to clear out the smoke," he reported.

Stella, coming up behind Carlo, heard this. Her face tightened with worry. "Carlo," she said, her voice trembling. "Another delay? We can't go on like this. Sherman's starting to talk about giving the account to another agency. McVie and Martin will fire me if I lose this account for them. My job is on the line—and let me remind you, so is yours."

Carlo spread his arms wide, palms upward, and shrugged. "What would you have me do?" he demanded. "*I* did not leave a plastic bag on top of a transformer."

"But somebody did," Bess whispered to Nancy. "I'm betting on that guy Miklos. We know he was there just before the fire. And judging from the way he looked at us, I'll bet he's still really mad at Carlo."

Nancy nodded absently. A few feet away in the crowd, she had just caught a glimpse of Stella's associate, Erik. The expression on his face looked strangely happy, as though he was very pleased with himself.

Was it possible that *he* was sabotaging the commercial, as a way of undermining Stella?

Just then Gayle came pushing through the crowd. "Hi, everybody," she said brightly to Nancy, Bess, Carlo, and Stella. "Isn't this exciting? I'm just glad that we'd finished on Paul Norman's set—I had time to get changed before the alarms went off. Can you imagine if we'd had to come down in pajamas? I would have died!"

Carlo nodded, staring oddly at Gayle. Suddenly he turned to Stella and said, "I have an idea. May I have a word with you?" He and Stella moved to the edge of the crowd.

Nancy glanced over at Erik again. He was looking after Stella and Carlo with a thoughtful expression on his face.

"You haven't seen my boyfriend, Jason, have you?" asked Gayle. "I lost track of him when we had to evacuate the studio."

"Sorry, no," Nancy said. "Listen, Gayle, we wanted to ask you—you were there this morning when Ms. Bowers got that call from the kidnappers, weren't you?"

"That's right," Gayle replied, looking disturbed. "I was *so* scared, I can't tell you. I mean, Ann's face practically turned gray. I thought she was going to faint!"

"You couldn't hear what the kidnappers were saying, could you?" asked Bess.

Gayle shook her head. "No, of course not," she said. "But I knew something had to be terribly wrong. And Ann told me everything the instant she got off. I could not believe it!"

Nancy nodded to herself. So at least Ms. Bowers had received the call, just as she said. After a moment's thought, Nancy asked, "Gayle? Aside from you, who are Cindy's friends in town? I'd like to get a better idea of what Cindy's state of mind has been lately."

"Let's see," Gayle said. "There's Aviva Sacks and Sally Wu . . . oh, yes, and Tiffany Lincoln. We all got started modeling at about the same time and kind of hang out together, you know?"

"Great. You don't know how I can get in touch with any of them, do you?" Nancy asked.

"As a matter of fact, Sally and Tiffany are both in a teen fashion show this afternoon at Way-bridge's, the big department store up on North Michigan Avenue," Gayle replied. "The reason I know is that I was asked to be in the show, too. But Ann had already signed me up for Paul Norman's shoot. I wouldn't have had time to take a runway job the same day. The fashion show was supposed to start at four."

Nancy checked her watch. "We can make it if we leave now," she told Bess. "Thanks, Gayle. We'll probably see you tonight at the apartment."

Gayle looked startled, then said, "Oh, right. I'd forgotten you're staying there. Okay, later."

As they walked away, Nancy said, "We'll be

better off taking the local El train than trying to find a place to park up near Waybridge's. We can pick the car up later.''

On the way to the elevated train station, Nancy stopped at a public phone and called Ann Bowers. When she got off, she told Bess, "Ms. Bowers knows the guy who's directing the fashion show this afternoon. His name's Andreas. She's going to call and ask him to let us backstage.''

"Do we tell the other girls that Cindy's missing?'' Bess asked.

"We'd better keep that to ourselves.'' Nancy said after a moment's thought. "We're simply interested in the teen fashion scene, okay?''

"Okay,'' Bess agreed. "But, Nancy, don't you think it looks more and more like Cindy's kidnapping is part of a plot against Carlo? I mean, that fire just now was no accident.''

Nancy nodded. "A plot against Carlo, or against the Healthibits campaign,'' she said.

"By Amalgamated Mills, for instance,'' Bess put in. "I bet that guy Miklos *is* working for them. Or maybe Paul Norman is. Didn't somebody say that he'd done a lot of commercials for them?''

"Doing commercials is one thing, setting fire to somebody's studio is another,'' Nancy pointed out. "Still, it *is* a connection to keep in mind.''

They found the entrance to the El. Despite its name—El was short for *Elevated*—in this part of town the trains ran underground. The girls walked down the stairs, bought tokens at the booth, and passed through the turnstiles.

As they reached the crowded subway platform, Nancy spoke the thought that was turning in her mind. "I wonder if Cindy really was kidnapped," she said.

Bess turned to stare at her. "*What?* But, Nan, we know she was! What about those phone calls?"

Nancy stepped out of the way of another passenger. "Look, I know this sounds crazy," she said. "But what if you decided to go away for a while, without telling anybody? If somebody else found out you were gone and felt really nasty, he could call your parents and announce that you'd been kidnapped, couldn't he?"

"I guess so," Bess said slowly. "I hope that's all this is—just Cindy going away by herself. But why would she do that without telling anyone, right before her big break?"

"I don't know," Nancy admitted. "Panic? Stage fright? It doesn't fit in with what we know about her. But maybe Cindy's friends can give us a clearer idea of her state of mind. I still think that may be the key to solving this case."

Bess shook her head, obviously unconvinced. Just then, the rumble of an approaching train stirred the crowd on the platform. As the train pulled in, brakes squealing, everyone edged forward.

Suddenly Nancy felt somebody press into her from behind. Was it just a commuter in a hurry, or was it a pickpocket, trying to distract her attention? She tried to turn around, but the surging crowd kept pushing her forward. She clenched her purse more tightly between her arm and her side. Nothing further happened.

Nancy stepped onto the subway car and looked around for Bess as the doors whooshed shut. Then she heard her friend let out a faint cry.

Nancy whirled around. "What is it?" she demanded. "Is something wrong?"

"Nancy, your jacket!" Bess gasped, grabbing on to a pole as the train gave a lurch. "Take it off and look at it!"

Puzzled, Nancy slipped out of her quilted satin jacket and held it up at arm's length. Then she caught her breath.

A jagged slit ran the length of her jacket, from the collar to the waist. It looked as if someone had gone at it with a razor—a deadly sharp one.

# 11

## Danger in Fashion

Nancy stared helplessly at her ruined jacket. She was only dimly aware that the train was pulling out of the station. Had the person who had slashed her coat boarded the train?

Suddenly alert, she tried to peer through the windows at the people left on the platform, hoping to spot a face she knew. But the train was already moving too quickly. She quickly scanned the crowd inside the train car. Again, there was no one familiar.

With a sigh, she went back to examining her jacket.

"Nancy, how awful!" said Bess.

"At least it was my jacket and not me" Nancy replied with a grim smile. "This time, anyway."

Bess's eyes widened. "You think it was a deliberate attack? Not just some crazy vandal?"

"I can't believe a crazy vandal just happened

97

to hit somebody who's investigating a crime," Nancy said. "That's too much of a coincidence for me. No, I think we just got a warning."

"So what do we do?" Bess asked uneasily.

"We go on with what we planned," Nancy told her. "Actually this is encouraging. Obviously we're getting close enough to the bad guys to worry them."

Bess put her hand through the long slit in Nancy's jacket. "They're getting close enough to us to worry *me*," she said. "How did they know we were down here?"

"Somebody must have followed us from Carlo's," Nancy said. She draped the damaged jacket over her left arm as she clung to a pole. "Somebody who knows what we look like. Which makes me suspect that we've already met the kidnapper—if it *is* a kidnapper—or at least one of his accomplices."

"Miklos?" Bess suggested. "When we saw him earlier, he looked mad enough to cut up somebody's jacket and the person inside it. And he certainly has it in for Carlo."

"He does now, since Carlo fired him," Nancy pointed out. "But why would he have kidnapped Cindy yesterday morning? Unless he was already working for somebody who wanted to sabotage the shoot."

"Like Paul Norman?" Bess said. "You did say that when we saw him in the hallway yesterday afternoon, there seemed to be another person there. What if it was Miklos, meeting secretly with Norman?"

Nancy thought for a moment. "Possibly," she replied. "But Norman isn't the only candidate. Like you said earlier, Miklos could be working for Amalgamated Mills. There's still something fishy about the kidnapping part, but at any rate, next time I talk to Carlos, I'll ask for Miklos's address and phone number so we can start investigating him seriously."

Two stops later, the girls stepped off the train and went upstairs to the street. The El station was right below Waybridge's, a big, top-of-the-line department store. They pushed through revolving doors into the elegant calm of the store's ground floor.

Just inside the entrance, Bess nudged Nancy and pointed toward a poster. Seaside Juniors, it said, over a stylized drawing of girls in summer wear. The Place on Three at Four Today.

"I wonder how many people tried to find the Place on Four at Three today," Bess joked.

Nancy smiled, then checked her watch. "Let's find Andreas before the show starts," she suggested.

They took the escalator to the third floor, then found their way through a maze of boutiques to The Place. A bank of lush green plants, strung with tiny white lights, separated the area from the rest of the store. Several people were already sitting at marble-topped tables set in front of a low stage with a short runway. Most of the crowd were teens, but there were quite a few women in their forties—probably moms, Nancy decided. On the stage, three rock musicians were adjusting their equipment.

A young woman in jeans and a striped boatneck tunic came over to Nancy and Bess. The name tag she wore read Jennifer. "Welcome to The Place on Three," she said. "Let me see if I can find you some chairs."

"That's okay," Nancy told her. She introduced herself and Bess, then said, "We're here to see Andreas. Do you know where we can find him?"

The hostess looked at them doubtfully. "I don't know—he's pretty busy, and the show's about to start," she said. "What's this about?"

"Ann Bowers was going to call him about us," Nancy replied. "We're interviewing people for a profile of Cindy Sunderland. She's a teen model."

"Sure, I know Cindy," Jennifer said. "We're all rooting for her to become a big star. I guess that's why you're doing this profile, right?"

"Right," Bess said. "And we want to talk to other teen models who know her. Can we go back to the dressing room?"

Jennifer shook her head. "Sorry, not until I check with Andreas."

The girls followed her across the room to the edge of the stage. Jennifer signaled for them to wait while she stepped up onstage and disappeared behind a pair of curtains at one side.

100

A minute later she reappeared, accompanied by a husky man with shoulder-length black hair and a bushy moustache. He wore a collarless shirt over black leather jeans.

"Ann Bowers tells me you want to talk to the models," he said, with a slight accent. "I'm happy to do Ann a favor—I owe her plenty—but you'll have to wait until the show's over, okay? You can watch from backstage if you like, but don't get in the way."

"We won't," Nancy promised.

She and Bess stepped behind the curtains and into another world. In contrast to the elegant scene out front, behind the scenes was a cramped space with scuffed white walls, lit by bare lightbulbs. Half a dozen gorgeous teenage girls crowded in front of a pair of full-length mirrors, chattering excitedly.

The girl nearest Bess and Nancy was dark-skinned, with short, curly black hair. She wore fire engine red flip-flops and a string bikini. She was talking to a pigtailed blond girl in a blue patchwork minidress and work boots. Behind them, in a white maillot swimsuit with a big yellow sunflower embroidered on the front, an Asian-American girl was carrying a pair of black swim fins.

Andreas clapped his hands and said, "All right, everybody, here we go. Just remember, think sun and fun. *Sun* and *fun*."

The band launched into an upbeat tune. Nancy

101

and Bess flattened themselves against the wall, as the girl in the bikini slipped over to the curtains. She slung an inflated inner tube over her shoulder and loped onstage, showing her perfect white teeth in an infectious laugh.

The Asian-American girl went after her, saucily swinging her diving fins at her side. Last in the group was a girl with a brown ponytail, in a tie-dyed two-piece swimsuit and white sandals. She held a red plastic pail and shovel.

Peeking through a gap in the curtains, Nancy and Bess watched as the three models circled the stage in a long-legged, hip-swiveling gait. They paused occasionally to pivot, giving the crowd an all-around view of their outfits. One at a time, they strolled to the end of the runway, where the audience could study their bathing suits up close. As the girls left the stage, the audience clapped loudly.

The other three models, in summer-weight cotton dresses so light that they seemed to float, strolled casually onstage. One carried a wicker picnic basket. Another had a red-checked tablecloth over one arm. The third was carrying a huge plastic ant. That got a big laugh from the audience.

Meanwhile, the girls who'd been wearing swimsuits sprang into a frenzy of activity as soon as they were back behind the curtains. A team of dressers pulled new outfits for them off a rack: shorts and microskirts in ragged denim, worn with bright halter tops, camisoles, or tie-front shirts. The dressers helped the models change swiftly.

"Notice how they step *into* their outfits, instead of pulling them on over their heads," Bess whispered to Nancy. "That's so they don't mess up their hairstyles and makeup."

"Yeah, but they still have that makeup artist checking them out before they go back onstage," Nancy said, pointing to a woman in a pink smock standing right behind the curtains. "These girls can change clothes completely in two minutes and look picture perfect. Why does it sometimes take you an hour?"

Bess sighed. "And even then I don't look as great as they do," she complained. "It must be because they're so thin. That does it—I'm going on a diet tomorrow."

Nancy shook her head at her friend. "Relax, Bess," she said. "You look just fine the way you are." Bess gave her a grateful grin.

Each of the models changed several more times. Nancy was amazed at the air of controlled chaos backstage. The show seemed constantly on the point of falling apart, but somehow everything got done just in time. Andreas was everywhere—adjusting one model's hairstyle, joking with another who seemed nervous, giving last-minute instructions to the woman operating the light board.

Thirty minutes later all the models went out

together and held hands for a bow. The drummer gave them a loud, crashing salute and the audience erupted in eager applause.

But as the girls filed offstage, Nancy saw the weariness around their eyes. No question about it, being a model was hard work.

Nancy approached the Asian-American girl. "Hi," she said, "are you Sally Wu?"

The girl smiled. "That's right. You're friends of Cindy's, aren't you? Andreas told us you were doing an article about her."

"Can we talk?" Nancy asked.

Sally nodded. "Tiffany and I are going over to the veggie bar as soon as we get dressed," she said. "Want to come along?"

"You bet," Nancy said.

Tiffany turned out to be the African-American who had opened the fashion show in a string bikini. In jeans and a big cotton roll-collar sweater, she looked like a different person. Bess and Nancy followed her and Sally to the veggie bar, a trendy little restaurant also on the third floor.

Once they were seated, Bess ordered a cranberry-carrot yogurt shake. Sally and Tiffany both asked for salads. Nancy ordered a bottle of mineral water.

"Well," Nancy said, once they had ordered. "We're researching this profile of Cindy, and we'd like your impressions. How did she feel about doing this new Healthibits campaign?"

"Thrilled," Sally said. "Scared," said Tiffany

104

at the very same moment. Then they both looked at each other and laughed.

"Thrilled *and* scared," Sally added. "But mostly thrilled."

"Did you get the feeling that anything was bothering her?" Bess asked.

"Sure," Tiffany replied. "She had a bad cold. I saw her last week, and she said she felt really miserable. She joked that if she didn't get well before the day of the shoot, she wouldn't know whether they were feeding her Healthibits or a bowl of sawdust."

Nancy was about to ask another question when she noticed Jennifer in the entrance to the veggie bar, scanning the crowd. She spotted Nancy and Bess and hurried over.

"There you guys are," she said. "Ann Bowers is on the phone for you. She says it's urgent." Nancy and Bess followed her back to The Place to take the call.

"Nancy?" Ms. Bowers said. Her voice trembled. "I just came back from the garage. Somebody smashed one of my car windows."

Nancy paused, stunned. "A thief?" she asked.

"No," Ms. Bowers replied. "I know it wasn't a thief, because he left a message for me. It was spray painted in big letters on the side of the car.

"It said, 'Stop meddling—or else!'"

# 12

## A Vandal at Large

As Nancy hung up the phone, she met Bess's questioning glance. "Somebody has been very busy this afternoon," she reported. "Ann Bowers just found a message painted on the side of her car—a warning to stop meddling."

Bess stifled a gasp. "Nan, do you think it's the same person who slashed your jacket?" she asked. "And who set the fire in Carlo's studio? Could it be Cindy's kidnapper?"

"Possibly," Nancy said. "If there *is* a kidnapper—which I'm still not convinced of."

"Well, one thing this tells us," Bess said. "Ann Bowers is not our culprit."

Nancy looked dubious. "It doesn't seem all that likely," she agreed. "But then again, she could have spray painted her own car to throw suspicion away from herself. Anyway, we'd better go look at her car. Maybe it'll give us a clue."

"Maybe we'll find another footprint of an Ourson running shoe," Bess suggested.

The girls hurried back to the veggie bar to settle their bill and to apologize to Tiffany and Sally for rushing off. Then they caught a taxi for the short trip to the apartment building on Lake Shore Drive.

They found Ann Bowers pacing back and forth in her living room. "Thank heaven I managed to track you girls down," she said as they let themselves in the front door. "I don't know why this incident has upset me so. It's just so malicious. I shudder to think of poor Cindy in the hands of people who'd do such a thing."

"Did you report the vandalism to the police?" Bess asked.

"Oh, yes, of course," Ms. Bowers said. "I had to—the insurance, you know. I'm supposed to go in later and fill out a form."

"Didn't they send anyone over here to investigate?" Nancy asked.

Ms. Bowers made a face. "The officer I spoke to offered to send someone," she said, "but I could tell he thought it would be a waste of their time. So I said not to bother. The police have so many more serious affairs to deal with, after all."

Nancy looked at her and wondered, More serious than menaces from an apparent kidnapper? She was about to ask the question aloud when the telephone rang. Ms. Bowers excused herself and disappeared into another room. When she returned, her face was pale and drawn.

"That was Cindy's mother," she reported. "Poor woman—she's handling her daughter's disappearance much better than I would, I'm sure. But the strain is really beginning to tell on her. She asked me if I think Cindy is still alive. Of course, I said yes. The alternative is . . . unimaginable."

Nancy shook her head sympathetically, then asked, "Do you have any way to pin down when the vandalism happened?"

Ms. Bowers thought a moment. "Not really," she said. "I had no reason to go down there earlier. But the man who parks in the next space lives on this floor, and I saw him coming home around three. If my window had been broken then, I'm sure he would have noticed and told me."

"So it must have been smashed sometime after three," Nancy said. She checked her watch—just past five-thirty. She couldn't believe what a long, event-filled day this was turning out to be. "What time did you discover the damage?"

"Around four forty-five," Ms. Bowers said.

"Is there a garage attendant?" Nancy asked.

"No, it's quite deserted," Ms. Bowers said. "I find it a little scary down there, to tell the truth."

Nancy frowned. "There's no security of any kind?"

"Well, access is very carefully controlled," Ms.

Bowers explained. "The only ways in are by elevator—which means you have to go past the staff upstairs—or through the driveway. There's a big metal gate blocking the driveway, and you have to have a key card to open it. Only residents are given those."

"You gave us one," Nancy reminded her.

"Well, of course, dear. You're my guests," Ms. Bowers replied.

"Gayle and Cindy are your guests, too," Bess said. "Do they have key cards?"

Ms. Bowers nodded. "Why, yes," she said. "But neither of them owns a car. They only use the garage when one of them rents a car for a weekend."

"Does Cindy usually carry hers?" asked Nancy. "If she does, her kidnappers must have it now."

Ms. Bowers looked startled. "I never thought of that," she gasped. "So *that's* how they got in."

"We should check with Gayle to see if she still has her key card," Bess suggested. "Is she home?"

Ms. Bowers suddenly seemed uncomfortable. "Uh, no, she's working this evening," she said, turning to look out the window at the lake.

"Still for Paul Norman?" Nancy asked, wondering about Ms. Bowers's abrupt change of manner.

"Oh, no," Ms. Bowers said, looking back at Nancy with a nervous little smile. "For Carlo."

Nancy exchanged a glance with Bess. Gayle was working for Carlo? Doing what?

"It was an emergency," Ms. Bowers continued. "The ad agency, McVie and Martin, is taking a lot of heat from the cereal company about the delay. I'm afraid they're considering invoking the escape clause in Cindy's contract, kidnapping or no kidnapping."

"Fire Cindy? That would be a disaster for her!" Bess exclaimed.

"I agree," Ms. Bowers said. "That's why I suggested an alternative. I don't know if you've noticed, but Gayle looks a lot like Cindy in build and hair color. Their features are different, but from the back you could easily mistake them. So I suggested to Carlo that he use Gayle as a stand-in for Cindy—just the parts that don't show Cindy's face, you understand. They'll be working late tonight, trying to get on schedule again."

Nancy thought that over for a moment. "Wasn't Gayle one of the top candidates for this job, before they finally picked Cindy?" she asked.

"Yes, she was," Ms. Bowers replied. She blushed and added, "I can guess what you're thinking. Gayle's my client, too—why should I care which of them has this job, as long as *one* of them does? But it's not that way, really it isn't. I'd never toss Cindy aside like that. Besides, I want her to be the Healthibits girl—she's perfect for the part, in a way that Gayle isn't."

"What happens if Cindy doesn't show up soon?" Bess asked.

Ms. Bowers winced. "Frankly, I don't know," she said. "I suspect McVie and Martin will try to use the escape clause. But if enough of the commercial has already been shot, that might sway them to take Cindy back when she returns."

"Or to give the job to Gayle?" Nancy suggested.

"It's possible," Ms. Bowers admitted. "Let me put it this way: If there's absolutely no way to save Cindy's job, then I hope Gayle gets it rather than some stranger. But until that happens, as far as I'm concerned, Cindy is still the Healthibits girl."

She sounded sincere, but Nancy couldn't be sure.

There were so many complicated pieces in this case. How did they all fit together?

"Can we take a look at your car?" Nancy asked. "Then we need to go back to the Film Center to pick up my Mustang. We can drop by Carlo's studio while we're down there."

"I'm in space C27 downstairs," Ms. Bowers said. "Do you mind if I don't come to the garage with you? I have to call the dealer to come get my car. They're going to have to repaint it, as well as replace the window."

"That's okay," Nancy assured her. "We'll see you later."

Ms. Bowers walked them to the door. "Good luck," she said. "And, oh—if you see Cody, would you ask him to give me a call?"

"Cody?" Bess asked, puzzled. "Why would we see him?"

"He called a while ago, to ask if there were any new developments. When I told him about substituting Gayle, he wasn't very happy," Ms. Bowers admitted. "He decided to go by the studio, to talk to Stella about Cindy's contract. Like a lot of law students, he thinks he knows everything." Ms. Bowers rolled her eyes.

Nancy frowned. "This call—was it before or after you discovered the damage to your car?"

"Oh, before . . . about an hour before," Ms. Bowers told her. "Why?"

"No reason," Nancy said, keeping her thoughts to herself. "We'll see you later, Ms. Bowers."

In the elevator, Bess asked, "Why did you ask her about the time of Cody's call?"

"Just an idea," Nancy said. "Remember, the message on Ms. Bowers's car said 'Stop meddling.'"

"Right," said Bess, still not getting the point.

"And Cody just found out that Ms. Bowers helped give Gayle a crack at Cindy's job," Nancy went on. "He'd certainly consider that meddling, wouldn't he? And he might have decided to give the meddler a warning."

"Does that mean you think Cody is behind all this trouble?" Bess demanded.

112

Nancy thought for a moment. "Not necessarily," she said with a sigh. "But with all these other incidents, maybe he thought he could get away with this one. He might figure that everyone would lump his crime in with the others."

"Very clever," Bess said, nodding. "Well, if Cody's still at Carlo's studio, we can ask him where he was between three and four forty-five."

The elevator doors slid open at the garage level, and Nancy and Bess went in search of space C27. Ms. Bowers's car, an expensive German sports coupe, was pale blue—except for the scrawled words in bright red. The clean cement floor on the driver's side sparkled with greenish fragments of safety glass from the window. The chrome door handles still gleamed, with no fingerprints evident.

"Ugh, what a mess," Nancy said. "Knowing Ms. Bowers's tastes, I really doubt she could do this to such an expensive car."

"The radio's still there," Bess reported, peering in through the broken window. "And it looks pretty expensive, too. So the motive wasn't robbery."

Nancy nodded, then slowly circled the car, studying it. How long would it take to spray four words, then smash a window? A minute? Less? And the culprit probably had his own car just feet away, ready for an instant escape.

"I don't think we're going to learn anything here," she decided. "Let's get over to Carlo's.

113

Whoever is behind all this is stepping up his mischief. If it's Miklos acting for Amalgamated— or Paul Norman—we'd better get some evidence on him fast."

The worst of the evening rush hour was over, so the cab ride to the studio was quick. Upstairs, no one seemed to notice Bess and Nancy come in.

They spotted Gayle in a chair having her honey blond hair styled. Her boyfriend, Jason, hovered nearby, running his fingers nervously through his short sandy hair. His broad-shouldered physique made him seem bigger than ever, with all these skinny fashion people swarming around.

Near the set, Stella and Cody were deep in conversation. Cody was waving his hands a lot. Carlo seemed in constant motion, with Charmaine scurrying along in his wake, taking notes on her clipboard. Nancy realized that it wouldn't be a good time to interrupt Carlo.

"Well, this is more like it!" Sherman Pike declared from the doorway. "It's a relief to see something happening at last, even if we have to pay overtime to get it done. I brought some Healthibits with me," he added, holding up an all-white cereal box. "If you all have to work through the dinner hour, at least you can have a healthy, high-energy snack."

He put the box on a table and crossed the room. As he passed Nancy and Bess, he smiled and nodded.

"What a change," Bess whispered to Nancy. "Yesterday he wanted us run out of town!"

"Is Erik around?" Sherman Pike asked Stella, breaking into Cody's monologue.

"He's at home in Lake Forest—done in by hay fever," Stella replied with an ironic smile. "I *think* we can cope without him."

Nancy blinked. Lake Forest? Why did that town name ring a bell?

But before she could think about it, Carlo called out, "All right, people. Let's try a run-through."

Everyone began to bustle toward the set.

Then suddenly, with no warning, the whole soundstage was plunged into darkness. The only light came from a red Exit sign, glowing eerily over the door. A panicky murmur began to rise from the crew.

"Now what?" Nancy heard Carlo shout angrily. "Who—"

Then above the hubbub rose a scream of terror.

# 13

## *Blues in the Night*

A second after the scream, a small flame blossomed in the pitch-dark studio, about ten feet away from Nancy. By its glow she recognized Sherman Pike holding his cigarette lighter just above his head. For one mad moment, she found herself thinking of the Statue of Liberty.

In the dim light Nancy then saw Gayle, still in her chair, with her face buried in her hands. Her shoulders were shaking. Jason was hurrying over to her from across the studio. He kneeled down and put his arm around her.

"Now we know who screamed," Nancy whispered to Bess. "Come on. Let's see if we can find out what happened."

Members of the crew had begun to shuffle around in the dark, groping their way by the shine of Sherman Pike's lighter. "Where's the electrical panel in this place?" Nancy heard Stella call out.

116

Just as Nancy and Bess reached Gayle's side, the lights came back on. Others in the studio noticed Gayle's distress and rushed over. "What is it? What's wrong?" various voices asked.

Looking up at the circle of spectators gathering around her, Jason barked, "Hey, c'mon, guys, give her some space, will you?"

Everyone took a small step backward, then immediately started inching toward her again.

Nancy leaned forward to listen as Gayle began to talk, her voice still trembling with fear.

"Somebody grabbed me!" Gayle was saying to Jason. "Right after the lights went out. I tried to pull away, but he held me tight. Then he kind of growled, 'What happened to Cindy can happen to you.' That's when I screamed."

"What happened then, Gayle?" Nancy asked.

Gayle looked up at her. "Why . . . nothing. He let go and sort of stumbled away."

"I'd just stepped away when the lights went out," Jason said. "I leave you for one minute, Gayle, and this happens." He clenched his fists with anger.

"Do you have any idea who it was?" Nancy asked Gayle. "Was there anything familiar about his voice, for instance?"

Gayle bowed her head. "No, nothing," she said, her voice rising. "Nothing!"

Carlo stepped between Nancy and Gayle. "Enough," he said. "Gayle, you have had a

117

shock. Go home, get a good night's sleep, and we will resume tomorrow morning."

Stella pushed forward. "Carlo, you can't!" she exclaimed. "Just when we'd found a way to move ahead with the shoot."

"Stella's right," Sherman Pike added. "We're so far behind already."

"After what has happened, you expect Gayle to perform at her best?" Carlo demanded. "No, no, no."

"Carlo, please," Gayle said anxiously, pushing herself out of her chair. "I'm ready, really I am. Look, Maxine and Ghalia did such terrific jobs on my hair and face. Why waste their work, and everybody else's?"

Nancy noticed the alarm on Gayle's face, as if she saw her big chance slipping right away from her. Was that what the saboteur had hoped would happen?

"We will all do even better work in the morning," Carlo replied. He patted Gayle's hand. "You will see. Now, home with you."

He looked over his shoulder at his film crew. "Eight o'clock call tomorrow," he said. "We have had much bad luck, but I have a feeling this will change. Good night and thank you."

People began to drift away, but Nancy and Bess stayed where they were. Nancy was busy measuring with her eyes the distance between the electrical panel, near the entrance to the studio,

118

and Gayle's chair. It was about fifteen feet, with no obstacles. After switching off the lights, the person would have been able to reach Gayle's chair quickly, guided by the faint glow of the Exit sign behind him.

"One person, acting alone, could have tripped the circuit breakers, reached Gayle's chair to threaten her, then faded into the crowd before the lights came back on," Nancy said to Bess. "That means that everyone in the studio is a potential suspect." Her eyes darted around the studio, noting who was there. "We didn't see Miklos around this time," she added in a low voice, "but that doesn't mean he didn't slip in and out without being seen. In this chaos, that would've been fairly easy."

"Gayle seemed to think it was a man, from his deep voice," Bess pointed out.

"Yes, but a woman could have lowered her voice enough to fool Gayle," Nancy said.

Charmaine came over and said, "Hey, guys, you got any plans? As soon as we can wrap it up here, some of us are going to a blues club. They have terrific barbecued ribs. You want to come?"

Nancy looked up eagerly. She'd been hoping for a chance to talk to Charmaine and the other crew members away from the studio. Maybe they could give her some useful leads on Miklos. She glanced over at Bess, who looked hypnotized by the thought of barbecued ribs.

"Great! Unless you've started your big diet already, Bess," said Nancy.

Bess poked Nancy with her elbow. "Tomorrow, I said," she declared. "So I'd better fill up tonight."

Nancy copied the address down from Charmaine and agreed to meet her and the others there in half an hour.

As she and Bess started toward the door, Nancy was amused to see that the box of Healthibits was no longer on the table. Someone on the crew must have decided that he needed a snack!

"Another delay," Bess was saying. "It's a good thing Erik wasn't here, or he probably would've blamed it on Stella. I wish he'd lighten up."

"Maybe he thinks it'll help his career if Stella looks bad," Nancy replied. "She's not really to blame, but—" Then Nancy stopped in her tracks.

"But what?" Bess demanded.

"Bess, didn't Stella just say that Erik was home tonight in Lake Forest?" Nancy demanded.

"Sure. With hay fever," Bess replied. "Why?"

"The shopping bag that started the fire here this afternoon came from a fancy store *in Lake Forest*," Nancy said. "Erik could have put it there on purpose, knowing it would melt and smoke up the studio. And what if he made the set fall over, too? We saw him hanging around there yesterday, right before it fell."

"So you think he's been trying to wreck the shoot, to make Stella look bad?" Bess said. "Sure, it all fits. But, Nancy, he wasn't here this evening. He couldn't have doused the lights and threatened Gayle."

"That's true," Nancy admitted. "But I still suspect he was responsible for that shopping bag stunt. Maybe the fire marshal could link the bag to him. We should pass on this tip, first thing in the morning."

After retrieving the Mustang from the parking lot, Nancy and Bess found their way to the blues club Charmaine had told them about. It was a couple of miles south of the Loop, in a brick building that looked like a converted garage.

Inside, long, narrow tables stretched out like fingers from the still darkened stage. Each table seated fifteen or twenty people on each side.

A side room held four brightly lit pool tables, all in use. At one, two young guys in baggy jeans and ragged football jerseys were playing intently. Their neighbors at the next pool table wore business suits and freshly shined loafers. "I guess this is a place for all tastes," Nancy commented with a smile.

"Hey, guys," Charmaine called. "Over here." She and some other crew members were sitting at a big round table at the back of the main room. Nancy and Bess pulled up two more metal folding chairs and sat down.

121

"We already ordered for you," Charmaine announced. "Ribs and fries. Is that okay? It's what they do best."

"It's about all they do," Maxine, the hair stylist, said with a laugh.

"That, too," Charmaine said, grinning. "Anybody orders the fried chicken, the kitchen probably has to send out for it."

While they waited for the food, Nancy chatted with the guy on her left, a sound engineer named Vinnie. He said he remembered seeing her that morning at Paul Norman's studio.

"At Norman's?" Nancy asked. "But don't you work for Carlo?"

"I freelance for lots of directors," Vinnie explained. He glanced around the table. "Most of us do. A producer like Carlo can't keep a bunch of techies on staff when he isn't filming."

"You must really get to know the business, working for different people all the time," Nancy said.

"Believe it," Vinnie replied. "It's a crazy racket, doing commercials. Like a roller coaster. Take Paul Norman—he was fit to be tied when Carlo got that cereal gig instead of him. But a few days later, he started getting more work than he can handle. Meanwhile, poor Carlo is stuck with a jinxed project. I hope it works out okay, though. Carlo's a nice guy, as well as a terrific director."

So much for Paul Norman's motive for disrupting Carlo's work, Nancy thought. "I was surprised to see Gayle taking Cindy's place this evening," she said casually. "Isn't that unusual?"

"You bet it is," Vinnie replied. "Right now, it's a break for Gayle, looking so much like Cindy. But in the long run, it may hurt her more than help her. Once Cindy's back, who'd want to hire an imitation when they can get the original?"

Just then the waitress arrived with plates of ribs, a platter heaped with french fries, and a thick stack of paper napkins. Bess's eyes were gleaming. They all helped themselves to fries and started on the ribs. Dripping with sauce, the ribs tasted fantastic, but they were unbelievably messy.

After a few bites, Nancy turned back to Vinnie. "Say, do you know that guy Miklos? The one who used to be Carlo's assistant?" she asked.

Vinnie took a sip of his soda, then said, "Yeah, but I don't really know him. What I've seen, I don't much like, I have to say. But I sort of feel sorry for him, seeing him hanging around the Film Center like a lost dog. I guess until he finds another gig, he doesn't have any place to go."

Before Nancy could ask any more, the band— two guitarists, a bass player, and drummer— finished tuning up onstage. Over the PA system, a deep voice said, "Ladies and gentlemen, let's have a big Chicago welcome for Spoonful of Blues!"

While the audience clapped and cheered, the band launched into what seemed to be its signature number, an old blues tune called "Spoon-ful." The table began to vibrate in time to the bass. Nancy decided to sit back and enjoy the music. Trying to talk to anyone was obviously out of the question.

The music was great, but Nancy felt herself fading by the end of the first set. She looked over and saw Bess give a huge yawn. It had been a long day for them both. They said goodbye to every-body and escaped outside into the quiet night.

As they drove north on Lake Shore Drive, Nancy told Bess what Vinnie had said about Paul Norman's recent hot streak. "Looking at it that way," she summed up, "Norman doesn't have much of a motive to sabotage Carlo." Bess agreed, with another yawn.

Nancy turned in at the garage entrance to Ann Bowers's apartment building. Digging the key card out of her purse, she slid it into the slot on a post outside the barrier. The steel door rolled upward, and she drove through into the gloomy garage. Most of the spaces were full. She followed the arrows to the guest slots and parked.

"What a day!" she said to Bess, as they walked across the concrete toward the elevator. "I hope we—"

Just then an engine roared behind them. Tires squealed. Nancy spun around.

Two blinding headlights were coming straight at them—*at breakneck speed!*

# 14

# The Puzzle Falls Together

"Jump!" Nancy shouted, as the car barreled down on them. She flung herself to the right and ducked behind a concrete pillar, then peered around. Bess had leapt to the other side of the aisle and was crouching behind the fender of a parked car.

The speeding car screeched to a stop, just a dozen feet away. Nancy could tell that the car was a medium-size dark sedan, but she was too far back—and the headlights were too bright—to see the person behind the wheel.

The car lurched into reverse and backed toward the entrance at top speed, gears whining loudly. Nancy ran out into the aisle and shaded her eyes, trying to see past the glaring headlights. At the far end of the garage, the dark car swerved and sped toward the exit.

"We must be getting pretty close to someone," Bess observed shakily, joining Nancy.

"Someone who knew when we'd be getting here," Nancy mused. "And someone who has a key card."

"Which means it's probably the same person who trashed Ms. Bowers's car," Bess said. "But who?"

Nancy smiled grimly. "That's for him or her to know and us to find out," she said.

Upstairs, the lights in the apartment were turned low. Ann Bowers had apparently gone to bed, and so had Gayle.

As they passed Cindy's room, Nancy noticed with surprise that the door was slightly ajar. She pushed it open and scanned the room. Everything looked as it had that morning. A draft must have blown the door open, she mused. But she wasn't convinced.

As soon as Nancy got up the next morning, she called Carlo at his studio to get Miklos's full name, address, and phone number. She also asked Carlo for the name and number of the fire marshal who'd investigated the fire the day before. When she dialed the marshal's number, a machine answered. She gave her name and number, then explained briefly about Erik's possible connection to the shopping bag. Now it would be up to the fire marshal to decide how to use the information.

While Bess showered, Nancy dressed and went

to the kitchen to put water on for tea. Ms. Bowers was sitting at the counter with a coffee cup. Crusts of whole wheat toast lay on a small plate in front of her. She looked as if she hadn't slept well.

"Before she left this morning, Gayle told me what happened at the studio last night," Ms. Bowers said. "How much longer can this go on? Cindy's been gone forty-eight hours now, and every hour brings new incidents. My nerves are just about shattered."

Nancy decided not to tell her what had happened to her and Bess in the garage late last night—it would only upset the woman even more. "We could call in the police," Nancy suggested.

Ms. Bowers squirmed uneasily. "Soon, perhaps—but not yet," she said, dodging the question.

"It's odd that we haven't heard from the kidnappers again," Nancy said casually. "That could be good, you know. If the kidnap call was just a hoax, there's still a chance that Cindy is unharmed."

"I hope so," Ms. Bowers said wearily.

"Ms. Bowers," Nancy went on, "do you think a company like Amalgamated Mills might hire someone to wreck a competitor's ad campaign?"

Ms. Bowers snorted. "Who suggested that— Sherman Pike?" she said. "He's read too many spy novels. Amalgamated would love to see Healthibits fall on its face, but they wouldn't do anything illegal. It wouldn't be worth the risk for them." She stood up and took her plate and cup to the dishwasher. "I'd better go. I do still have a business to run."

A few minutes later Bess appeared, with a towel around her head and a puzzled look on her face. "That's funny," she said. "I decided I'd like to have some Healthibits for breakfast, so I went to Cindy's room to get the sample box. But it was gone."

"It must be really good stuff," Nancy commented. "People can't seem to resist it. The box that Sherman Pike brought to the studio last night vanished, too."

Then she paused, wondering. Why had two boxes of Healthibits vanished—one from Carlo's studio and the other from Cindy's bedroom? Was it just a coincidence, or did it mean something?

Nancy reached for the phone and called Carlo's studio again. Charmaine answered this time. Nancy asked if Sherman Pike was there.

"No, he had stuff to do at his office today," Charmaine said. "Want me to give you that number?"

Nancy scribbled down the number Charmaine gave her, then called Sherman Pike. He agreed to see Nancy and Bess in half an hour.

Bess hurriedly dried her hair and, grabbing a

128

banana muffin for breakfast, headed down to the garage with Nancy. By the light of day, the place looked much less forbidding than it had the night before.

The two girls drove to Sherman Pike's office, which was downtown in the Loop. When they arrived, he was on the phone. He nodded hello and pointed to two chairs. When he hung up, he said, "Well, girls, the mystery is solved."

"It is?" Bess said, astonished. "Cindy has been found?"

"Well, no, not exactly," said Pike. He took a cigarette from the pack on his desk and lit it. "But that was Stella Laporte. Erik Johansen has just confessed that he was the one trying to wreck the shoot."

Nancy just stared at him.

"Apparently he caused that fire yesterday," Pike went on. "He sabotaged the set the day before, too. When the fire marshals went to his house and questioned him this morning—on a tip from you, I understand—he broke down and told them everything."

The cereal company executive blew a cloud of tobacco smoke across the desk. Nancy turned her face and had to cough. Too bad the fire marshals couldn't take care of Pike's cigarette!

"I guess Erik was hoping the delays would make Stella look bad," she said. "And he was obviously willing to take a risk. That set wall

129

nearly fell on him, too! But what about the lights going out last night? Erik wasn't there then. And most important, what about Cindy?"

"Erik swears he had nothing to do with Cindy's disappearance," Pike said. "In fact, it wasn't until she vanished that he got the idea to cause more delays."

Nancy looked over at Bess with wide eyes. With Erik's confession, a big part of the case was solved, but Cindy was still missing. That meant that her disappearance *wasn't* connected with the sabotage at the studio.

Sherman Pike continued. "But tell me, girls, what did you want to see me about?"

"This may sound silly," Nancy said. "But we didn't get a chance to try any Healthibits last night. Do you have some around?"

Pike looked at her shrewdly, guessing that there was more to her request than met the eye. "Of course," he said. Swiveling his chair, he opened a cabinet and took out another of the white boxes. "I'll ask my secretary to find some bowls."

"Oh, don't bother," Nancy said. She poured some of the cereal into her palm, passed the box to Bess, and took a small taste. It wasn't bad— like granola, but with a hint of orange and carob.

"I like it," she told Pike.

"So do I," Bess said. "But I liked the other version better. The one with crushed nuts."

Pike frowned. "You must be thinking of some

other product," he said. "That's one of our selling points, in fact. Most health-food cereals do have nuts, but you'd be amazed at how many people dislike nuts. Lots of people are even allergic to them. For them, Healthibits is the answer—it has all the advantages of a healthy cereal, but with no nuts."

Bess frowned stubbornly. "But I like nuts," she said. "And I'm positive that there were nuts in the box of Healthibits that Cindy had at her apartment."

Nancy felt her jaw drop. She flashed to an image of all those allergy medicines in Cindy's bathroom. What if that other box *had* had nuts in it—and Cindy was allergic to nuts?

"May I use your phone?" Nancy asked urgently.

Pike pushed it across the desk. "Feel free."

Nancy quickly called Cindy's mom. "Mrs. Sunderland," she asked, "is Cindy by any chance allergic to nuts?"

"Why, yes," Mrs. Sunderland replied. "She has to be very careful. If she eats anything with nuts in it, her face swells up something awful. It's not painful, and her doctor insists it's not usually dangerous, though of course it depends on how much she's eaten. But it's scary all the same. And you can't be a model if your face looks like a balloon, can you?"

"How long do these allergy attacks usually last?" Nancy asked.

"It depends," Cindy's mom told her. "Sometimes it's as long as three days before the effects wear off. Nancy, where *is* Cindy? Is she all right? I've been worried sick. I spoke to Ann Bowers again this morning, but she said she couldn't tell me anything new."

"I can't make any promises," Nancy said. "But I think I'll have good news for you by this evening."

When she hung up, Nancy saw that both Bess and Sherman Pike were staring at her. "This evening?" Pike said. "Are you really that close to finding Cindy?"

"I hope so," Nancy said.

Pike leaned back and clasped his hands behind his head. "So do I," he said. "Watching that other girl, Gayle, last night, I realized that I agree with Stella—Cindy is the ideal spokesperson for our product. Get her back for us, please."

"We'll do our best," Nancy promised, getting to her feet. "Thanks for your cooperation."

In the elevator going back downstairs, Bess said, "So Cindy is violently allergic to nuts. Nancy, I *know* there were crushed nuts in that box of Healthibits in her room."

"I believe you," Nancy replied. "But how did they get there?"

"The box was open," Bess recalled. "And remember? Ms. Bowers said she found a cereal bowl by the sink when she came home from the theater. Cindy must have tried the cereal that evening."

"And the next morning, she vanished," Nancy went on. "If the cereal did have nuts, when she woke up her face would have been swollen completely out of shape. Suppose she decided to run away, rather than risk losing the job with Healthibits?"

"I guess that would make sense," Bess said. "But what about the rest of it? The kidnapping calls and all the threats?"

"I'm not sure," Nancy admitted. "There are still a lot of pieces to put together."

As they stepped out of the elevator, Nancy strode briskly across the lobby. Despite Bess's questions she felt enormously relieved. If Cindy had simply disappeared because of an allergy, then their biggest worries were over.

But as she reached the big glass doors, Nancy halted, frowning. "But how did those nuts get into Cindy's cereal, Bess?" she pondered. "What if someone put them there deliberately?"

"You mean like a practical joke?" Bess asked.

"Not a very funny joke," Nancy declared. "Serious allergies can be very dangerous. What if Cindy's throat swelled closed, or she went into anaphylactic shock and her heart stopped?"

"Nancy!" Bess stared at her in horror.

"I'm not saying that's what happened," Nancy added hastily. "But it's possible. And if the person responsible for her death found her, he or she might have hidden the body somewhere, hoping that the crime would never be discovered."

"Cindy dead?" Bess said, her eyes filling with tears.

Nancy shuddered at the thought, then reached over and patted her friend's shoulder. "Let's hope not," she said. "If she *is* alive, then she's probably in hiding."

"Where do you think she might be?" Bess asked as they pushed through the doors.

Walking down the street, Nancy tried to imagine herself in Cindy's situation. If she had to disappear, wouldn't she want to have help from someone she trusted? A close girlfriend, like Bess—or her boyfriend?

"Maybe there's someone who does know where she is," Nancy said. "Do you still have Cody's address?"

Bess stopped to rummage through her wallet. She soon found the address. It was on the west side of Chicago, out toward Oak Park.

"Let's go," Nancy said, setting off at a jog for the parking lot to get the Mustang.

Twenty minutes later they were parking in front of Cody's apartment building. "Keep your eye on the door and your fingers crossed," Nancy told Bess. "I'm going to try to trick him into leading us to Cindy."

Nancy went to a pay phone on the corner and called Cody. He picked up on the second ring.

"Hi, this is Nancy Drew," she said. "Look, Cody, I'm getting really upset. Stella told Ann Bowers this morning that she's decided to give the Healthibits job to Gayle. For some reason, they don't believe Cindy was kidnapped, they think she just skipped out."

After a silence Cody said, "I can't talk now, Nancy. I'll call you later."

Nancy hurried back to her car and motioned for Bess to slide down in the seat. A minute later they saw Cody rush out of his building. He got into a white compact car. As soon as he pulled out, Nancy and Bess followed, half a block behind him.

For the next hour Nancy used every trick she knew to keep Cody from spotting them. He led them north for miles, into the forests of Wisconsin, on smaller and smaller roads. Nancy had to stay far back, out of sight, and often she couldn't see Cody's car. Eventually, as she rounded a bend, what she'd been dreading happened.

"Nancy! We've lost him!" Bess exclaimed.

"Not yet, we haven't," Nancy replied grimly. "Maybe he saw us and sped up, but maybe he just turned off somewhere. You watch your side and I'll watch mine."

A hundred yards farther along, Nancy suddenly hit the brakes. "Look!" she said in a low voice.

A track led off to the left, into the woods. A branch that overhung it was still swaying, as if something had just brushed past it. Nancy pulled off the road on the opposite side, hiding the Mustang behind a thick cover of bushes. "From here we hike," she announced.

She and Bess followed the track through the woods. In five minutes they reached a clearing. Through the trees, a pond sparkled in the sunlight. Cody's car was parked at the edge of the clearing, near the foot of a muddy, bramble-choked path.

"Nancy, look!" Bess exclaimed, pointing at the ground next to the white car.

In getting out, Cody had stepped in a patch of mud. Nancy instantly recognized the shoeprint. It was an Ourson running shoe—size ten.

# 15

## The Island's Secret

As she looked down at the incriminating footprint, Nancy felt her thoughts spin. So Cody had been the eavesdropper they'd chased into the basement freight tunnels. And it had been Cody who'd pushed the Dumpster at them yesterday.

That meant that Cody was willing to resort to violence. What if *he* was the one who had doctored Cindy's cereal, hoping an allergic reaction would force her to give up the Healthibits campaign?

Was this place Cindy's hideout? Or her prison? Or her grave?

"It was Cody who attacked us!" Bess said indignantly. "He must have been afraid that we'd find out the truth."

"It looks that way," Nancy agreed. "But that wasn't his car that tried to run us down in the garage last night. His car's a white compact. The one last night was a dark sedan."

"He must have borrowed another car or stolen it," Bess retorted. "We'd better be careful. If he spots us, he could be dangerous."

Nancy took the lead, following the narrow path through the trees along the edge of the pond. The air was still and humid, and soon she felt a trickle of sweat on her face and neck. A cloud of tiny bugs hovered around her head, too. She tried to brush them away, but it was like trying to wrestle mist.

Then Bess tapped Nancy's shoulder and whispered, "Look—a tiny island with a cabin on it."

Nancy peered through the screen of trees. The island, not much bigger than a tennis court, was about fifty feet from shore. A swaying footbridge linked it to the bank. The cabin was small, too—no more than two or three rooms. A deck jutted out over the water, looking like a perfect place to spend a lazy afternoon pretending to fish.

"They must be inside," Nancy whispered back. "Let's be quiet—we don't want Cody to know we've found them."

The two girls crept along the path until they reached the footbridge. At this end, the ropes that supported it were tied to a sturdy oak tree. Bess examined it, then gave Nancy a questioning look.

Nancy pointed to herself, then toward the island. She stepped onto the bridge, moving carefully from plank to plank and gripping the cords that served as handrails. Once across, she turned back and beckoned to Bess.

Bess took each step as if she expected it to tip her into the water. Reaching the island at last, she whispered to Nancy, "Never again! I'd rather swim!"

"You won't have to," Nancy whispered back, pointing to a small boat with an outboard motor tied up nearby. "We can borrow their boat instead."

Nancy and Bess crept up to the cabin. There was a tiny, square window about six feet to the left of the door. They approached it cautiously and peered inside.

Nancy heard Bess gasp.

Inside was a rustic living room with a hardwood floor and knotty pine furniture. Cody, his back to the window, was talking earnestly to a blond girl with a round, moonlike face and swollen eyes. In a moment Nancy realized with shock who it was.

Cindy!

At that same moment, Cindy looked past Cody at the window. Her eyes met Nancy's. Her eyes met Nancy's. Her mouth flew open in alarm.

Cindy said something to Cody, who looked quickly over his shoulder and saw them. He sprang for the door. Looking around, Nancy spied a pile of firewood and grabbed a piece. She braced herself, ready for a fight.

Cody came charging out the door. He skidded to a stop when he saw Nancy brandishing the wood. "Whoa," he said, holding up both palms. "We don't want a fight. We need to talk to you."

"Go ahead," Nancy said, ready for anything. "Talk."

Cody glanced around nervously. "Can we go inside?"

Nancy nodded warily. Cody reentered the cabin, with Bess and Nancy right behind him. As they crossed the porch, Nancy tossed her piece of firewood on a stack of logs, next to a rusty ax and a red metal gasoline can for the motorboat.

Cindy came running over to greet them. "Oh, I'm so glad to see you," she cried, throwing her arms around Bess, then around Nancy. "This has been such a nightmare, I can't tell you."

It occurred to Nancy that Cindy could have seen them anytime, if she'd simply come out of hiding. "It's been rough for a lot of people," she said. "Carlo, Ms. Bowers, your mom . . ."

"I don't know how I'll make it up to everyone," Cindy declared, tears brimming in her eyes. "But I will, I swear!"

"Cindy, what happened to your face?" Bess asked sympathetically. "It's an allergy attack, right?"

Cindy stepped backward, flushing with embarrassment. "Let's sit down," she said. "I'll tell you the whole story."

There were chairs near the fireplace. Once

they were settled, Cindy started. "When I woke up the day before yesterday," she said, "I knew I couldn't let anybody see me. You must think I look grotesque now, but this is nothing compared to that morning. I didn't even think, I just ran."

Nancy nodded toward a pink stuffed pig propped up on the table. "Taking Wilbur along, I see," she noted.

"I figured I needed all the good luck I could get," Cindy admitted. "So I crammed him into a shoulder bag, with a toothbrush and a few clothes, and caught the train to O'Hare."

"The airport?" Bess asked, surprised. "Why?"

Cindy shook her head. "I don't know," she said. "I guess I was thinking about flying somewhere far away. But when I got to the airport, the first thing I saw was an ad with my picture on it. That's when I realized I couldn't run away— people would surely recognize me. So I decided to hide instead."

"When you called me that morning, Nancy, I had no idea where Cindy was," Cody added. "But she called me from O'Hare a minute later. I drove up to get her as fast as I could, then brought her here to my uncle's weekend cabin."

"Which one of you thought up the kidnap hoax?" Nancy asked.

"Me," Cody admitted. "When I found out about that escape clause in the contract, I realized that Cindy couldn't simply drop out of sight. So I called Ann Bowers and pretended to be a kidnapper. Then I went over and said I'd got a call, too."

Bess said, "We spotted you eavesdropping at Carlo's studio and chased you into the freight tunnels."

"How did you know it was me?" Cody asked, amazed.

"We saw your footprint on the stairs," Nancy told him. "You left the same print when you tried to crush us with that Dumpster."

"What?" Cindy demanded. "Cody, what is she talking about?"

"They tracked down your herbalist," he told her. "I was afraid they'd figure it all out. So I decided to distract them. I knew they'd have time to get out of the way. Dumpsters don't roll very fast."

"Was that why you slashed Nancy's jacket on the subway, too?" Bess asked, giving him a steely look. "To distract us?"

He stared at her. "I don't know what you're talking about." Nancy studied his face. He seemed sincere.

"Look, none of this really matters anymore," Cindy said miserably. "I've had time to do a lot of thinking out here, and I've decided I have to give up the Healthibits campaign."

"Cindy! Why?" Bess protested.

"How could I film a commercial, eating Healthibits?" Cindy explained. "I'd swell up on the first take! Besides, I couldn't sell a product I'm allergic to. I'd be living a lie."

"But, Cindy—" Nancy started to say.

"What hurts most is how they lied to me," Cindy went on, getting more and more worked up. "I asked, you know. I asked Stella if Healthibits had nuts in it. She told me it didn't. I didn't say why I was asking—I pretended I just didn't like nuts. But why did she lie to me like that?"

"She didn't!" Bess broke in. "Healthibits *doesn't* contain nuts. We confirmed that this morning with Sherman Pike."

"Then what made my face swell up?" Cindy demanded. "I had a bowl of Healthibits the other night, and the next morning I looked like something from a horror movie!"

"The box in your apartment *did* contain nuts," Nancy told her. "Bess tried some, and she tasted the nuts. But they must have been added after the box was opened. Somebody played a very dirty trick on you." Nancy found herself looking over at Cody. His expression showed obvious surprise.

Cindy jumped up. "You mean I can do the campaign after all? That's fantastic!"

Cody was still taking in the news. "Who would do such a thing, Nancy?" he asked.

Cindy had already grabbed Wilbur and started for the door. "Who cares, Cody?" she declared. "What are you waiting for? I've got to get back and explain to everybody. I just hope they can forgive me for running away."

She grabbed the wrought-iron door latch and tugged. It didn't move. "It's stuck," Cindy said, confused. "Or locked."

"It can't be locked," Cody said, joining her. "There's a hasp for a padlock outside, but the padlock is over there on the mantel."

He, too, tugged at the door. It didn't budge.

Nancy got up to help. But as she moved past the window, a sharp whiff of gasoline caught her nose.

Nancy ran to the window and looked out. An orange glow whooshed up, flickering against the bushes around the cabin.

Nancy tried to keep her voice very calm. "We'd better find a way out, right away," she said. "Somebody's set the cabin on fire!"

# 16

## Ablaze!

The smell of gasoline gave way to the smell of burning wood. A little trickle of gray smoke drifted in under the bottom of the door. Cody gripped the handle with both hands, braced one foot against the wall, and heaved. The door didn't open.

Cindy stood in the center of the room, clutching Wilbur in her arms and breathing shallowly. Nancy was sure she was about to faint. "Bess?" Nancy said in a low voice. "Take care of Cindy. I'll look for a way out."

The three windows in the living room were high and small. Cody had pushed a table against the wall, under one of them, and was trying to climb out the narrow opening. He got his head and shoulders through, but he couldn't go any further.

Meanwhile, behind a curtain, Nancy found a door that led onto the deck. She tugged at the

145

knob, but it wouldn't budge. The upper half of the door was four small panes of glass. Nancy took one step back, swiveled on her left foot, and kicked out with her right. One of the windowpanes shattered, and the thin wooden frame cracked.

She kicked again and again, smashing the rest of the panes. By then Cody had joined her. He wrapped his jacket around his hand and knocked out the jagged pieces of glass that still remained.

"Okay, everybody, let's get out this way!" Nancy shouted. Cody helped Cindy and Bess climb through the waist-high opening. Then he hoisted himself out and turned back to help Nancy. The narrow deck hung out over the water, but one end was just a couple of feet from the island. Nancy climbed onto the railing and jumped the gap, then offered a hand to the others.

In seconds everyone was safe on dry land. Nancy ran to the front of the cabin, looking for a hose, a bucket, or anything to help fight the fire.

At the corner of the house, she skidded to a stop. "Hey, it's not the cabin that's on fire," she called to the others, who were hurrying up behind her. "It's the footbridge!"

Several planks at the near end of the wooden bridge were burning as well as the wide poles the supporting ropes were lashed to. Before Nancy and her companions could do anything, the flames ate through the ropes. The bridge sagged and then fell into the water, with a hiss of steam.

"Someone's trying to trap us on the island," Nancy said.

"How do we get off?" Cindy wailed. "I can't swim!"

Cody gave her a quick hug. "Don't worry," he said. "There's still the motorboat."

Nancy inspected the front door of the cabin before joining the others in the boat. "No wonder we couldn't get out," she told them. "The intruder stuck a thick stick through the steel loop where the padlock usually goes. We could never have forced the door open from inside."

After half a dozen jerks on the starter cord, Cody got the outboard motor going. Two minutes later, they were scrambling out near the narrow path that led back to the clearing and Cody's car.

Cody moored the boat to a tree, and then took the lead. As they reached the clearing, he let out an angry yell. "I'll strangle him!" he shouted. "Just give me two minutes alone with the creep who did this!"

Nancy looked past him to see what was the matter. All four tires on Cody's car were flat. Deep gashes on the treads showed that someone had gone at them with a knife.

Cody jerked the door open and looked inside. "He stole the cellular phone, too," he announced. "*Now* what will we do?"

147

"Maybe my car is okay," Nancy suggested. "I left it out of sight on the other side of the road."

The four teens jogged down the dirt track to the highway. Nancy's convertible was still where she had parked it, and the tires were still fine.

"Whew! He didn't see it," Bess said gratefully.

"Either that, or he was in too much of a hurry to damage it," Nancy said as she unlocked the doors. "Or maybe he thought the jammed door and burned bridge would be enough to keep us out of his hair."

"Or maybe he tampered with the motor," Cody added grimly as he hopped in. "Check it out, Nancy."

Nancy slid into her seat and tried the ignition. The Mustang started at once. "Next stop, Chicago!" she called.

As they pulled onto the road, the teens speculated about who had followed them to the cabin. "I assume it's the same person who put nuts into your cereal, Cindy," Nancy said. "But the way this crazy case has been going, you never know." She quickly filled in Cody and Cindy on Erik Johansen's confession to the incidents at Carlo's studio.

Then Nancy asked Cindy more questions about the box of cereal. Who had had the opportunity to add crushed nuts to it?

"I brought it home that afternoon," Cindy explained. "It was the first sample the company had given me, so I was eager to taste it. I ate a little bit then, and nothing bad happened. Then, before I went to sleep, I wanted a snack, so I took it to the kitchen and poured out a bowlful."

"And you put the box back in your room?" Bess asked, turning from the front seat to face Cindy.

"Not right then," Cindy remembered. "I felt really restless, so I went out for a long walk."

"The nuts must have been added while the box was in the kitchen, during the evening," Bess said. "Who was in the apartment during that time?"

"I know Ann was at the theater by then," Cindy said. "I don't know where Gayle was."

Nancy looked at Cindy in the rearview mirror. "Who has keys to the apartment, besides you, Ms. Bowers, and Gayle?" she asked.

"Why, no one," Cindy replied. She leaned forward, eyes wide. "I see what you're getting at. Ms. Bowers couldn't have done it, so it must have been . . . Gayle! But that's awful. She's my friend!"

Cody pounded the wall of the car with an angry fist. "That traitor!" he exclaimed. "I always thought she was jealous of your success, Cindy. But she acted like Miss Sweetness and Light when you were around. You're too trusting sometimes, Cindy."

"We don't have any proof that Gayle is behind this," Nancy warned him. "But the pieces do seem to fit. She could have taken the incriminating box from Cindy's room yesterday, if she

149

thought we were getting close. And she could have hidden the box Sherman brought to the studio yesterday, too."

"But it's hard to imagine Gayle chasing us in that car last night, or vandalizing Ms. Bowers's car," Bess remarked.

Nancy shrugged. "Well, we'll know soon enough," she said, stepping harder on the accelerator.

Once in Chicago, Nancy parked near the Film Center. As they got out, Nancy nudged Bess and pointed down the street to a dark midsize sedan. Bess nodded. "I can't be positive," she said, "but it sure does look like the car that chased us in the garage last night."

Going up in the Film Center's elevator, Nancy suggested, "Let me and Bess go in first."

Cindy nodded. She looked very serious and a bit scared.

Charmaine let Nancy and Bess in the door. "We're just taking a break," she said. "Today's been pretty hard work, but thank goodness, no more accidents."

Entering the studio, Nancy spotted Gayle and Jason standing together near the set. Jason's head jerked up as he saw Bess and Nancy. He turned to Gayle and whispered something. She peered over at Nancy and Bess and frowned.

"Carlo?" Gayle called. "I'm really sorry, but I don't think I can work with all these outsiders in the studio. Nancy, you understand, don't you?"

"I understand better than you think," Nancy replied. She turned toward the door and called out, "Come on in!"

Cindy walked in, followed by Cody.

Both Carlo and Stella recognized her at once, despite her swollen face. "Cindy!" they shouted.

Gayle gasped and reached out for Jason's arm.

"I'm back, Gayle," Cindy said firmly. "Your nasty plot didn't work. Gayle, how could you!"

Gayle burst into tears. "I didn't mean any harm," she sobbed. "It was supposed to be a joke!"

"You knew Cindy was allergic to nuts, didn't you?" Nancy asked Gayle sternly.

"Yes, she told me," Gayle said faintly. "And then Jason and I were kidding around about it, you know? Like, what if Healthibits really had nuts in it and she tries it on the set and blimps out? We were goofing around, that's all. Then the other night, we go up to the apartment and find a sample box of Healthibits on the kitchen counter, open."

"So you put crushed nuts in it," Bess said. "Knowing it would make Cindy's face swell up."

Gayle bit her lip and refused to answer.

Nancy pressed on, "Then, when Cindy vanished and we started investigating, you made a threatening phone call to us, and you slashed my jacket. You spray painted Ms. Bowers's car to pay her back for calling us back on the case, and you tried to run us down in the garage last night."

151

Gayle looked blank. "No, I didn't," she said, pouting. "All I did was fake being attacked last night in the studio, when Jason turned off the lights. We wanted to give everybody a scare. After all, everyone was so worried about Cindy— and not about me!"

"But this morning you followed us to the country and tried to trap us there," Bess concluded.

"I didn't!" Gayle declared. "I've been here in the studio since eight this morning. Ask anyone!"

She swallowed hard, and continued. "And I didn't put the stuff in Cindy's cereal. I joked about it, sure. But that's all."

As Gayle's statement sank in, everyone in the room turned to stare at Jason. For a long moment, he stood there, shoulders back, jaw clenched, glaring. Then he made a sudden dash for the door.

"No way, buddy!" Cody shouted. He sprinted after Jason and made a flying tackle. Jason crashed to the floor and lay there, stunned.

Nancy turned to Carlo. "I think you'd better call the police," she said.

After Jason and Gayle were taken away by the police for questioning, Cindy went to Carlo's office to call her mother. When she returned, her cheeks were stained with tears, but she looked relieved.

Ann Bowers came hustling anxiously into the studio. "Carlo, where is she?" she asked. Seeing Cindy, she ran over to give her a hug. "Cindy, dear, it was terribly thoughtless of you to make us all think you'd been abducted," she rattled on. "Your poor mother has been worried sick these past three days."

"I know," Cindy said contritely. "But look at my face. What could I do?" Then she sighed. "It was dumb, I agree. I ran away, hoping to save my career. And now, running away has *ruined* my career."

Stella broke in. "Not at all," she said. "Sherman Pike and I still want you to be the Healthibits girl. Why, we could even work your nut allergy into the script. What better way to show how healthy Healthibits are?"

"The filming will wait until your swelling goes down," Carlo said. "Which will be tomorrow, right?" he added optimistically.

"I hope so," Cindy said, giggling with relief.

"Jason has confessed to everything," Nancy reported from her brief conversation with the police. "He still claims the whole thing was just a series of pranks that got out of hand. He says he'll pay for my jacket and Cody's tires and the damage to Ann Bowers's car. But he'll still face charges for vandalism and reckless endangerment."

Carlo turned to Nancy and Bess. "You two girls

have pulled off a miracle," he proclaimed. "Tell me—have you ever thought of appearing in commercials? I am sure I could use your talents."

Bess threw him a sparkling, eager glance. And, looking around at the crew and the set and the whole crazy, glamorous scene in the film studio, Nancy paused for a second, too. For a moment she felt tempted.

Then she shook her head, laughing. "No thanks, Carlo," she replied. "It's a lot safer being a detective!"